WILDER

PENNY CHRIMES

WILDER

Illustrated by Manuel Šumberac

Orion

ORION CHILDREN'S BOOKS

First published in Great Britain in 2023
by Hodder & Stoughton

5 7 9 10 8 6

A CIP catalogue record for this book is available from the British Library.

ISBN 978 1 510 11071 7

Typeset in Horley Old Style by Avon DataSet Ltd, Alcester, Warwickshire

Printed and bound in Great Britain by Clays Ltd, Elcograf S.p.A.

The paper and board used in this book are made
from wood from responsible sources.

Orion Children's Books
An imprint of
Hachette Children's Group
Part of Hodder & Stoughton Limited
Carmelite House
50 Victoria Embankment
London EC4Y 0DZ

An Hachette UK Company

www.hachette.co.uk
www.hachettechildrens.co.uk

For Reginald Braithwaite Chrimes.
Who never stopped fighting for a better world.
Never forgotten, Dad.

PART ONE

The child – if child it was – came naked out of the wild-ness.

It came out of the sparse bleak marsh beside the village where few dared go and none came back.

'No good ever came from that place,' is what the villagers said. 'The marsh takes and takes and never gives back.'

For the slither of marsh silt and the creep of marsh grass had been stealing the shining river from the villagers and their fishing boats lay idle and rotting in the mud. They were bitter people and narrow as the barren strip of land that was all they had left.

Some women, rising early to draw well water, found the child standing alone at the edge-lands on a winter's dawn.

It was staring at the huddled houses with such hunger in its eyes.

'As if it would devour us all,' went the whisper between them.

Its shock of hair was the yellow-white of the blast-bleached grasses – a colour not seen on the dark heads of these villagers – and as coarse and tangled as briar brambles. Its legs were scarred and marked with swirling patterns like lashings and stings. And the sounds it made were the sounds of the wild wind, as if it had never before heard the speech of man.

The women crossed themselves with superstition-born fear and called their men, who would have driven the child back into the wild-ness from which it came.

But a mother, whose son had walked into the marsh one moonlit night and never returned, pushed her way between them and put her arms about the child. Like a fledgling fallen from a tree, it shrank into her softness and nested in her emptiness. Its black eyes were watchful as the unblinking glare of the falcon that wheeled high, unseen, above its head.

'She has been sent by the river,' the mother said. She was known as a Wise Woman who saw things beyond seeing, and her green eyes flashed a challenge to any that would argue.

'I shall call her Rhodd*,' she said and the name was soft as breathing between her lips.

'Wrath?' muttered one, because that is the way the name sounded to their ears. And why – after all – would you call a child 'anger'?

'It means "gift",' the mother replied, but in what deep and ancient language she did not say.

And so the villagers grew accustomed to the creature and allowed that it was a girl, for the sake of their own peace of mind. But they did not forget from where Rhodd came.

And they whispered that there was no knowing whether she was sent as a blessing or a bane.

---

* Pronounced 'Roth'

Go safe, child.

Hide from its eyes until you grow strong.

But never forget your wild-ness within.

Nor the wild-ness without.

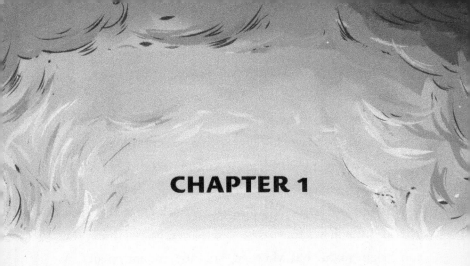

CHAPTER 1

'A is for Apple, B is for Book, C is for Cat, D is for Dog, E is for Egg . . .'

Rhodd yawned. Was it worth a scolding from Ma for escaping her chores, just for such dull stuff as this?

In her sun-pooled hiding place behind the schoolhouse, the drone of bored boys blurred with the drone of a bee. Distracted, Rhodd shifted her gaze from her stolen alphabet book to the bee's eyes – and she saw in that instant exactly as the bee saw.

Gone were the soft muted shades of the spring flowers, the gentle pinks and blues of the campions and the columbines. There was now a brilliance at the throat of every flower, unseen by the human eye; a brilliance that seduced the bee into the very heart of the bloom. The flower dazzled the bee's five eyes, dusting its fine hairs with grains of golden pollen like tiny suns.

Try that one, Rhodd told the bee and it changed direction and followed her nod with a buzz of thanks.

The bee began to drink itself daft on nectar. Rhodd was swaying, her senses blurred.

'Enough!' Rhodd pulled her eyes back from the bee's eyes and shook her tousled head impatiently, rewilding the sun-bright mane that Ma tried daily to tame into plaits. A flurry of small creatures scattered from her lap – timid mice and whiskered voles and long-nosed shrews that had gathered about her skirts for the crumbs she brought from breakfast. But it wasn't Rhodd they were fleeing. A dark wide-winged shadow had fallen from above.

She lifted her gaze to the cloudless sky.

'There you are!' she breathed, though she had no need of words with him. Wheeling high in the blue skies, almost beyond human sight, was her falcon and her eyes were now his eyes, sweeping and scouring the earth below. Clean, clear, knife-sharp. Savage. No creature crept or flew beneath that fierce gaze without his knowing. Some he let live.

An invisible thread stretched between falcon and girl, a thread that had never broken since Rhodd had walked out of the marsh on a winter's dawn, all those years before. That thread anchored her, still, in the wild-ness, even though she had no thinking memory of what her life had been before she came here. Three years old – that had been her mother's guess about how old she was when she arrived at the village. But by what magic she had reached that age, nobody knew. Nor what she had been escaping.

Through the falcon's eyes she saw the village below, laid out like a faded, tattered ribbon along the skirts of the marsh. One long street – with houses only on one side – leading to nowhere. For that is what this place had become. Nowhere. Nobody came here from the country beyond. There was nothing to come for, with the river gone.

Midway along the street stood the pub, next to the village green. It had once been a busy coaching inn but only moths slept in its beds now. Behind it, the cobbled square of the stable yard no longer echoed with the sound of horses' hooves – her falcon-ears could hear only the creaking of rotted half-doors on broken hinges. The next strong wind could take them off but nobody cared enough to lift a finger to mend them.

Even now, with the sun barely dipping from its noon height, there was a cluster of men leaning against the walls of the pub. As if the effort of standing was too much trouble. 'Lazy do-nowts,' Ma called them, lips pursed in disapproval, but the truth was that there was nothing *to* do since the marsh had swallowed the river.

This desolate place had once been a thriving port, where boys went out to sea as sailors or stayed home and lived a good life from the fishing. But when the river left them, so did the fish and now the marsh barred the way to the sea.

A huddle of bedraggled houses slouched along what had once been a busy riverfront, full of cries and calls and bustling travellers and tradesmen. Their bleary windows stared past the ribs of boat skeletons and out over the blank expanse of flat marsh. No man's land, where no man went who planned to come back. On a winter's night you could hear the pale ghosts of those who had ventured too far, wailing with the wind. But the doors and shutters of their old homes were barred tight against their return.

At the dead end of the street, like a pair of outcasts, stood a couple of cottages even more ramshackle than the rest. One of those cottages was the place Rhodd called home. And from the sky her falcon-eyes spied Ma standing outside the door. Hands on hips, elbows bristling.

'Rhodd! Where are you? Plague take the child!'

Even from the other side of the village, tucked behind the schoolhouse, Rhodd's falcon-ears could hear the impatience in that voice. Impatience over chores left undone, dishes left dirty, floor left unswept.

'Ma . . .' Rhodd scrambled guiltily to her feet, sending a last vole scurrying for shelter in the long, sweet-smelling grass. The alphabet book tumbled to the ground. She sighed and picked it up. No matter how hard she studied it – and she *did* study it hard, because she hated to be outdone by numbskull boys – the shapes of the letters written on it meant nothing to her.

How could 'A' be for apple, when 'A' looked like nothing but the distant blue hills? How could 'O' be for owl when 'O' was the sun or the fat full moon above her head? 'W' was easier, because that was waves made by wind on water, and she was prepared to allow 'T' to be a tree with bare branches stretching below the sky . . .

But these words – owl, sun, moon, waves, tree – they were not her words. In Rhodd's head, there was no need for language for such things. They just were and always had been. Ageless and of the earth.

She felt the falcon soar away and leave her, and her heart dropped back into her chest, earthbound once more.

'I wish . . .' But the wish was too big for words.

She longed to soar with him, envied him the wind beneath his wings. The air was his element. She ached to escape this human body and fly, to free-wheel on the air currents, up and up towards the sun. But she always turned her head away when he flew out over the marsh, always snatched back her gaze before she could see that whole wild expanse spread beneath.

She was not ready to remember the truth of that place. Not yet. Even though she knew in her heart that something waited for her out there, brooding. And that one day she must face it.

A fluttering and anxious tweeting and twittering from the beech hedge stole Rhodd's attention back from the sky. Between the shimmering fresh green of the new leaves poked the head of a sulky little bundle of barely grown feathers. A mother sparrow followed, nudging her reluctant fledgling out of the nest that was hidden deep in the tangle of branches.

The baby bird teetered nervously out on to a thin branch, which it clearly did not believe for a moment could hold its weight. It was still almost as much fluff as feather, and as Rhodd watched, it ruffled up the fluff and gaped its wide mouth to make itself seem more helpless. It was clearly hoping that its mother might change her mind and feed it and then that they could go back to the cosy nest. Instead of this horrible misunderstanding that it was time for it to fly.

Rhodd switched her gaze to the fledgling's gaze, saw through its eyes the dizzying drop to the ground. She could feel all the little bird's terror and bewilderment over being ousted from a safe warm world with a steady supply of worms.

Be brave, Rhodd told it. **You can do it, you're ready. You must have courage!**

It fluttered its untried wings, wobbled, panicked. **No, I can't, I can't . . .**

You can! I know you can!

And then, quite suddenly, it could.

Rhodd gasped as the fragile framework of blood and feather and bone trusted, against all reason, that the empty air would hold it. It fluttered, flapped. Caught a wing-hold on the breeze. And flew.

She lay back to watch the mother sparrow supervising her baby's first unsteady flights. Rhodd had been holding her breath with the fledgling – now she smiled. **I told you that you could do it.** But it was already gone, rejoicing in its new-found freedom.

The freedom to fly . . . Ah! How she envied it.

A bell rang. Rhodd didn't need her falcon's eyes to know that a dozen village boys were tumbling out of the front door of the schoolhouse, eager to escape. All shapes and sizes. All looking for some smaller creature to pick on, after hours of struggling with their lessons.

A slick of quick sweat made her shiver – she was normally so careful to be gone before now. She shoved the precious schoolbook under her smock. She had stolen it a few weeks before from one of the boys, and she'd grinned with her sharp little white teeth as she'd listened to him taking a scolding from the schoolmaster for losing it.

A sound gathered in the girl's throat that was closer to a snarl than anything human. By instinct, life was a matter of fight or flight for Rhodd.

Her fingers flexed like the talons of her falcon. But experience told her she could not take on the village boys when they hunted in a pack. And Ma had said she must stop fighting or they would both be driven from the village.

'Rhodd! What you still doing here?' A head, shaggy with dark hair, peered round the side of the sandstone building. 'You need to get gone, quick, afore they find you!'

CHAPTER 2

The hissed whisper had come from a boy a little taller but even skinnier than Rhodd. He glanced behind him before darting round the corner to join her. He often found her here, listening to the lessons she wasn't allowed to join.

'Come on – we need to scarper – the Johnsons are all riled up 'cos they got the cane for spitting on the floor . . .'

Rhodd scrambled fast to her feet, pulling down the long smock to hide the dark marks on her legs. Even Gar, her best – in fact, her only – friend, had never seen them. The strange scars hadn't ever faded since she walked out of the marsh, in spite of her mother's physicking, and Ma had warned her to keep them hidden under her skirts from curious eyes. Clothes had been a battle between her and

Ma in those first weeks. The wild child had torn them, snarling, from her back and fled outside to roll naked in the mud until the smell of them was gone from her skin. But in the end, she'd learned she must wear them, like she'd learned so much else.

'They've no more wits between them than a coot, them three,' Rhodd sneered.

Gar was used to the slight halt in her speech that made it sound like she was translating from another tongue. The village children called her 'slow top' – amongst other insults – but the truth was that her instincts flew ahead of human thoughts, too fast to turn into words.

'Don't reckon they care much about wits, the Johnsons,' Gar replied now. 'Got fists for brains, that lot.'

Rhodd nodded. Gar was right. Two fists each. She didn't need to go to school to know that made six. And even the smallest of the Johnson brothers was twice her size. At least that's how it felt.

'What'll us do, Rhodd?' Gar gazed at Rhodd with complete trust. They were like two halves of a whole. He was the practical one, the clever one. But she was the one with the wildest ideas. A perfect partnership. He'd never known Rhodd fail to get them out of a scrape. Or, at least, almost never.

Rhodd shrugged. 'Dunno.' But a grin twitched at the corners of her mouth.

Something flickered, deep, savage, in her fierce black eyes. That something made Gar shiver sometimes, even though he'd known her for so long and she had never once turned her savagery on him. Her irises were so dark you couldn't see the pupils and so large you never saw the whites, but he was used to that as well. Even the bright yellow rims of her eyelids beneath her dark lashes didn't bother him. It was just one of the things that made her different, and Gar liked different.

Gar was the only child in the village who'd ever been allowed to play with the wild girl. The rest of the mothers reckoned they'd done enough by not driving the strange creature back where she had come from. The truth was, they feared her, and they'd brought their children up to fear her too. They'd never got over the suspicion that she was somehow linked with the marsh, the marsh that had swallowed their river and was killing their village.

Rhodd and Gar had grown up as neighbours, always in and out of each other's homes. Like Rhodd and her ma, Gar and his mother had been pushed to the edge of the village – to the most ramshackle cottages that nobody else wanted – because they were different. Because

Gar didn't have a pa. Or at least no pa who would admit to him. And his ma had never told him who his father was, not even whether he was dead or alive. She kept that secret close.

Rhodd and Gar could hear the shouts of the boys larking about in the street, pushing and shoving one another in trials of strength. But they were evenly matched, all of them. It was only a matter of time until they got bored and looked about for a smaller victim to pick on.

'Where's that teacher's pet snuck off to?' someone shouted. They resented Gar because he was smarter than any of them. He could even read, which most people in the village regarded as the nearest thing to witchcraft. None of the other boys bothered to pay attention to their lessons. They knew their parents cared as little as they did for learning.

'He'll be off with mud girl . . .'

Rhodd planted her feet firm, pulling courage up from the earth like a tree pulling water from its roots. Wary, alert. If she'd had whiskers, they would have been twitching. She knew Gar had risked a beating by coming to warn her – he could have just sneaked off home without checking she was safely gone. But the pair of them always stuck together. They always had.

The one-room schoolhouse was a square sandstone building at the opposite end of the long village street from Ma's cottage. It was the old customs house, but nobody used it for trade now because no ships came here any more. Since nobody needed it, the man who owned the village, Lord Stanley, had begrudgingly paid for an out-of-work schoolmaster who wanted to move in and run it as a school. But the villagers had no faith in learning – and they certainly wouldn't waste it on their daughters, who were kept home to do chores. They saw it just as a way of keeping the boys occupied and out from under their feet.

Immediately behind the schoolhouse rose steep sandstone cliffs that loomed over the whole length of the village. All the houses in this one-street village faced out over the marsh, with the cliffs at their backs. The only way home for Rhodd and Gar was down the high street. And past the gang.

Gar watched Rhodd's face. He knew she saw things he did not see. He recognised the almost imperceptible twitch about her yellow eyelids now, as she cast about for an escape.

Rhodd's focus had fallen on one of the mice that had benefited from her breakfast crumbs. She needed to borrow its eyes, to see what her enemies were doing.

I need a little favour, she asked the mouse.

Rhodd did not have to speak out loud – and in fact her conversations with creatures never took on the form of words in her mind, but rather mind-shapes that floated between them.

If you wouldn't mind . . .?

The creatures of the village had long cradled and protected Rhodd, ever since she walked out of the wild. They were well used to helping her out of trouble. Besides, the mouse was an obliging creature, and it had enjoyed the crumbs. It nodded, and in a moment it was scurrying along the side of the schoolhouse, towards the boys.

Without question, the mouse allowed Rhodd to use its eyes, to see what it saw – and in that instant grass stalks became tree trunks and hummocks of soil became hills. Mouse nostrils snuffled in damp earth and mouse whiskers brushed against daisies and dandelions. Even after Rhodd had lost sight of the creature, she saw as the mouse saw and heard as the mouse heard.

At the front of the schoolhouse, the little animal hid under a large dock leaf to watch the boys. Four of them – giants to the mouse's eyes – had gathered in a gang around the three brothers. The Johnsons were always the ringleaders.

They smell of danger, the mouse told Rhodd.

'Where's Mister Clever-Clogs gone?' one of boys was saying.

'We'd have seen him if he'd headed home. He can't have gone far. He'll be with her . . .' Another of the boys nodded round the corner. 'Marsh girl hides back there . . . I has seen her skulking about . . . spying on us . . .'

Mouse ears twitched. Rhodd mused idly to herself that mice's ears were really much too big for their tiny bodies. They were like great saucepans fastened to their heads. But this was no time to waste on thoughts like that. She lifted her head and looked at Gar. 'They're coming.'

The boys' heavy boots crunched towards them, down the side of the schoolhouse. The mouse fled. Rhodd snatched up a dead branch, pronged with brittle branches.

'Run, Gar,' she whispered. 'Round the other side.'

'I ain't leaving you, Rhodd!'

They both knew it was too late to run anyway. And the boys would outrun them, even if they did.

'There you are, mud worm!'

The Johnson brothers stood at the front of the gang like three identical clothes pegs, in descending order of size. All barrel-chested, narrow-hipped, with little eyes gawping out of red cheeks, under mops of greasy black hair. The

Johnsons were the only family in the village well off enough to keep a pig, and they were living proof of the old saying that people always ended up looking like their animals. Although to Rhodd's certain knowledge pigs were a lot kinder than the Johnsons. And cleaner.

Rhodd's hands clutched into claws, holding her nails ready. Rage rose in a snarl and growled low in her throat until Gar nudged her. 'No, Rhodd – remember what your ma said.'

She sighed. Forced herself to find words. 'Idiots! Numbskulls! Clodpates! Nick-ninnies!' These were words Rhodd liked and collected. She could see the point of them. She could hurl them like weapons.

The largest of the brothers took a step closer. 'Marsh girl!' he yelled. His breath stank like bad fish.

'I'm not a—' Rhodd's retort was lost as a frog chose that moment to hop out of the pocket of her smock.

Startled, the boys took a step back.

Rhodd's vision flickered for a moment. Frog eyes saw nothing but sheer stone as it leaped towards the walls of the schoolhouse. Clammy frog skin sensed damp . . . water . . . safety.

Where are you going? she asked the frog.

Follow me . . .

The youngest Johnson brother, seeing something small and helpless, stuck out his foot to squash it beneath his boot.

'No! Don't . . .' Rhodd screamed and shrank away as if it was her own body that was about to be crushed. But then she felt a thrust of energy surge through her own body as the frog's powerful back legs propelled it towards the long grass at the bottom of the wall. The boy's foot stamped down on nothing.

Rhodd stood tall and laughed at the boys' baffled faces. The frog was gone.

Gar stared at Rhodd. He was as baffled as the rest of them.

'Down there, Gar. Follow the frog.' Brandishing her stick like a weapon at the eyes of the closest Johnson boy to keep him back, she shoved Gar down on to his knees behind her, towards the spot where the frog had disappeared.

Gar wriggled into the thick clump of grass at the bottom of the school wall. He was guessing at the way the frog had gone. A gap appeared in front of him. It was the opening to a rainwater drain – and it was just wide enough to crawl into.

'Go on,' Rhodd urged. She gave him a gentle kick of encouragement.

'There's nothing down there but . . .'

The gang gaped as Gar vanished, head first. Rhodd was already flat on her stomach wriggling backwards after him, still brandishing her stick at the boys like a sword.

Gar's wail was swallowed in a splash from below. '. . . water!'

CHAPTER 3

Small and skinny sometimes had its advantages, even if it came from never having quite enough to eat.

Crouching up to their ankles in a drain full of muddy water, Rhodd and Gar could hear the Johnsons and their followers snuffling and snorting with frustration above their heads. There was no way they would be able to squeeze down that opening.

Rhodd held herself very still. She was trying to breathe, trying to keep down the panic born of being trapped under the earth. She had always hated not being able to see the sky.

In those early days, after she had first walked out of the wild, it had been many months before Ma could persuade her to sleep indoors. Each dawn Ma had woken to find

Rhodd's little bed empty and found the child curled up outside with Ma's dog, Red, where the pair had slept the night under the stars.

'It's not that *I* mind where you sleep, Rhodd,' she'd told the silent solemn-eyed girl. Ma instinctively understood how hard it was for her to breathe indoors, shut in between walls and under a roof. 'But we have to think about what *they* say . . .' And she had jerked her head towards the village.

She'd added under her breath, '*If* you're to stay.' Something had always told Ma that was a big 'if'. She knew Rhodd was a gift that could one day be taken back. And she knew that one day she might have to face losing another child to the marsh. She had never forgotten the son who had disappeared into that dark wilderness.

Water was trickling down Gar's face now and he sneezed mud out of his nose. Head first had not been the best way to come down.

One of the boys picked up Rhodd's stick and poked it down the drain opening, trying to get at them. Rhodd seized it and gave it a sudden strong tug, enough to overbalance whoever was holding it. She and Gar sniggered at the boy's squeal of fright.

'Leave 'em,' the biggest Johnson said at last. 'Down

in the muck, where they belong.'

Mutters of agreement. 'Need to get back for us dinner, anyhow, or we'll get another hiding off Ma.' The sound of retreating boots came from above, as the boys scuffed and kicked at stones in frustration at losing their victims.

Rhodd felt a brief twinge of sympathy for the brothers. If they weren't being caned at school, they were taking a beating at home. Their father was the landlord of the pub, an angry red-faced man who took out his disappointment over his lost profits on his family. It felt like the grown-ups were always angry in this place, apart from Ma. No wonder their children were constantly on the lookout for someone they could beat up themselves.

She herself had never known anything but gentleness from her mother, no matter how much it had cost Ma in the eyes of the village. She'd folded her arms about Rhodd like the great wings of a swan whenever the strangeness of this world was too much for her, even when the child spat and growled and clawed at her in those early days. She had contained Rhodd's savagery in calmness, until Rhodd had learned to contain it for herself. Or mostly, anyway.

The twinge of sympathy didn't last long, and it was quickly replaced by a twinge of guilt. She'd left Ma with all those chores. 'It's time to go. Ma'll be worried.'

Gar snorted. 'Easy to say, Rhodd. We're stuck down a drain.'

His brilliant blue eyes glinted with laughter in the shaft of daylight from above. They both giggled. They'd faced worse scrapes than this together. And at least the gang was gone.

Gar pointed at a dim circle at the end of the long wide pipe stretching ahead of them under the school. It was veiled by green ivy.

'Reckon they put this pipe down here for drainage – it must go under the building and then under the road,' he said. Rhodd stared at him blankly. Gar loved stuff like that, people-made things. Stuff that she could make no sense of, things for which her mind had no language.

'The downpipe takes the rain off the roof up there,' he tried to explain. 'Then the rain runs into the drain an' out through this pipe – out to the – to the marsh . . .' Gar tailed off, doubtful. Every child born and bred in that village had been taught never to step foot on to the treacherous wilderness of the marsh.

Ma's son, Rhys, was not the only child to have disappeared on a moonlit night, never to be seen more. Every year a child had gone missing – another had gone just a few weeks before on the first full moon of the spring. It was as if they were drawn out on the flood tide of the distant sea. The marsh was still taking from the village. It was like an angry god demanding its annual sacrifice. And for the villagers it had become a place of superstitious dread.

Rhodd looked quickly away from that green ivy circle. It was instinct, not women's warnings, that kept *her* from the marsh. She couldn't remember what made her fear it, but fear it she did.

Not that way, she thought. *Never that way.*

Where was the frog? In the low light, Rhodd caught the slimy shine of the creature's bulging eyeballs. It was holding itself in stillness until it was sure that danger had passed. She switched her gaze to the frog's eyes. It was looking towards the faint circle of light in the distance.

Not the marsh, she told it. **Show me another way . . . I cannot . . .**

In fact, 'I dare not,' was closer to the truth of how she felt.

If frogs could shrug, this one seemed to shrug its moist shoulders in reply. It sighed. **Nothing better to do, I suppose.** Rhodd found that most frogs she had met tended to be of a lugubrious, melancholy disposition.

Perhaps it went with being permanently damp.

With characteristic swift suddenness, the frog turned its eyes away from the marsh and leaped up the drain, back the way it had come. On the way down, that slope had seemed to Rhodd like a sheer drop. But looking through the frog's eyes – which worked better than her own in the dim light – she spotted layers in the sandstone rock. In fact, now she saw with his eyes, there were plenty of small crevices and cracks for foot- and handholds.

She passed on her thanks, but the frog was already gone. His job was done, he'd kept Rhodd safe. And she knew – because he'd mentioned it to her – that he was looking forward to a large slug he had spotted up there that would do nicely for his lunch.

'This way,' she told Gar, and set off to clamber after the frog.

Out of a lifetime's habit, Rhodd glanced to the sky when she emerged from the drain a few moments later. Her falcon was there, hovering like she had known he would be, as if poised for a death-bringing dive. His face was a grim-set, moustachioed mask, black beside the brilliant yellow around his savage beak; his eyes were glittering black pools circled by the same brilliant yellow, and his chest and underwings were banded black and cream. But when he wheeled away, satisfied at the sight of her, his upper wings shone blue as if they had been cut from the cloth of the cloudless sky.

People had a word for him, as they had for all things, it seemed. *Peregrine*, they called him. She had learned that people loved to name things, as if it was a way of owning them. But Rhodd did not own her falcon. In her mind he meant *freedom*. But that was an idea with a shape that soared and swooped through her thoughts. Not a hard, narrow word.

'"Peregrine" means wanderer, pilgrim, someone who never stops travelling,' Ma had told her years ago, thinking that Rhodd needed a name for the creature she watched so intently. 'A foreigner who is always away from their home.' And the strange child pulled her black eyes quickly down from the sky as if she had been caught in something so secret, she could not share it even with Ma.

'Race you!' cried Gar now, and he tore off round the schoolhouse and into the street.

Rhodd tore after him, still clutching her alphabet book to her chest. *Ma'll be so proud of me, one day, if I can only make sense of those shapes*, she'd always told herself. She hadn't once let go of it – had kept it safely tucked under her arm – even when she'd tumbled into the drain.

At the front of the schoolhouse the pair checked quickly that the gang was gone, and then hurtled towards their homes at the other end of the high street. They'd learned a long while back that it was better to run. A moving target was harder to catch and thump.

Rhodd chased Gar along the low wide wall of red sandstone slabs that divided the village from the marsh. This was the old quayside, where centuries of footsteps – both booted and bare – had worn away the top of the soft stones into smooth shallow dips. Rhodd and Gar could judge to a nicety when and how far to leap over the gaps, where gangways had once been lowered to allow passengers off great seagoing ships. Ships carrying wealthy travellers who'd stayed at the inn and brought money to the town. But that was before the river went away, before the children's knowing.

Now and then Rhodd's glance slipped sideways towards the marsh, where the wind rippled through the reeds as it had once whipped up waves on the river. Innocent-seeming patches of reflected blue sky were the only clue to the deep ditches and gullies. The screams of the grey gulls sounded like the shrieks of desperate drowning men.

There was a restlessness to that desolate landscape. The channels constantly changed; they were never to be found in the same place for long, they could never be trusted. Come back the next day and they'd be gone. On a grey day – or a dark night – there was no seeing them until it was too late.

Rhodd dragged her eyes quickly back to the path in front of her. She always kept her senses firmly shut to the creatures that clung to life in the marsh. She did not want to listen to what they might tell her.

But she could not help hearing the thud of the great wings of swans departing as she ran. They sounded like fading heartbeats. And the wind shifted, restless, amongst the reeds, and keened in mourning for the lost river.

Open your eyes, child.

Open your ears.

Listen to the call of your wild heart . . .

The time is coming.

CHAPTER 4

It wasn't just her own ma standing outside the pair of ramshackle cottages when Rhodd arrived home with Gar. Gar's mother, Bethan, stood next to Cerys, and both had their arms folded ominously tight over their chests.

'Where've you been 'til now?' Bethan whipped out a hand to her son and cuffed him around the ear. 'School finished an age back.'

'It wasn't our fault,' wailed Gar. He was dancing and hopping to keep away from his mother's reach, trying to talk himself out of trouble. He was good at that. Rhodd sidled past the pair of them and bent her head repentantly to her own ma.

'Sorry, Ma,' she whispered. 'The Johnson brothers caught us an' we had to hide.'

Cerys just sighed. 'What happened to your plaits?' She pulled Rhodd's head close and kissed her, smothering a soft whisper in her wild mane. 'What's to become of you . . . ?'

Rhodd glanced quickly up into Ma's face. She wasn't sure she'd heard her right. Why did she look so worried? Time was when she would have treated Rhodd to a scolding every bit as bad as Gar was getting, but all Rhodd could see now was grey weariness. It was much worse than a scolding.

Ma was shivering, despite the sun's heat. 'Come, Rhodd. You've chores to do.'

Ma's dog Red was lying across the threshold to the cottage. He lifted his shaggy russet head to glare reproachfully at Rhodd as she followed Ma, then lowered it back down to his paws with a snort of disapproval.

Sorry, Red. Rhodd squatted down and pressed her head to his square forehead by way of an apology.

Red had been her first friend in the strange new world she'd found herself in all those years before. It was between his paws she had curled up and taken refuge, when her mother first brought her home. It was Red who had first warned Rhodd that she was different. And that she must take care.

When she'd first left the marsh, Rhodd never questioned the way her senses slipped between the creatures of the earth. When she was out walking with Ma in those early days – her mother holding her little hand tight, as if she thought Rhodd might slip away like her own lost son – she didn't think twice about shifting her gaze and adopting another animal's senses. It happened without conscious thought. She was still more part of their world than she was part of the human world.

One moment she might be looking out of the eyes of a cat plotting the murder of a sparrow, the next she was slithering with a grass snake, tasting on her tongue the tempting scent of a cricket balanced on a blade of grass. In those days she happily chattered out loud in her own wild tongue, conversing with every creature she met. Sometimes she even warned the sparrow or the cricket that they were about to be eaten, although she instinctively knew she should not take sides in the wild world.

'Hush, Rhodd!' Her mother had always shushed the infant's strange chatter nervously because of the hostile glances she was attracting in the street. 'It doesn't do to be different in these parts.' Rhodd never spoke her mind-shapes out loud again.

It was on those long nights lying out with Red beneath

the stars, before she consented to sleep in a bed, that the dog had made Rhodd understand the dangers of this human world. She'd been gurgling in delight as she used the dog's sharp ears to listen to the bats squeaking jerkily after moths, and his eyes to watch the barn owl whooshing ghost-like towards the moonlit marsh. But then came his warning.

You are in their world now, he told her. **You must hide what you are – and hide what you see – and hide what you know.**

Oh, but it was not with words that he warned her, never with words! Mind-shapes floated soft as mist between the child and the dog without ever becoming anything so solid as words.

After Red's warning, Rhodd had fallen silent for many months until her mother despaired of her ever speaking. Her conversations with the wild world continued – she did not need to speak out loud to talk to other creatures. But at last, Rhodd forced her mind-shapes into human thoughts and forced her tongue to lick those thoughts into human words. And she spoke.

Now, all these years later, Rhodd saw herself through Red's brown eyes and she didn't much like what she saw. She stood up and looked round the dark little one-room cottage. Dishes unwashed, floor unswept, and barely enough wood left to keep the fire alight. She had let Ma down.

'Shall I make tea, Ma?' Her mother was still shivering.

Ma nodded and sank on to one of their two remaining chairs. The rest they'd burned for firewood last winter, as the bitter wind howled off the marsh and battered at their door. Red pulled himself up and padded over to Ma. The old dog sank into a warming heap over his mistress's feet to stop her shivers.

Rhodd hesitated before approaching the fireplace and forced herself to pick up the poker. Holding her body as far from the fire as possible, she jabbed at the glowing embers under the kettle and then stepped back quickly with a gasp, as a flame leaped up like a living thing.

Fire was an untameable thing in Rhodd's mind. Earth, water, air – these were elements she knew and understood – but fire she always approached with fear. When her mother first brought her home, she'd wailed and shrunk from the hearth in terror until Ma caged the flames behind a guard. Even now she did not really trust that fire was an element that could ever be made safe, an element that she could ever control.

Rhodd reached for a jar and carefully measured out some dried herbs. They called it tea, but in truth it was whatever herbs Ma could gather or grow.

Cerys was watching her. 'Your pa—' She stopped, corrected herself. 'He wasn't *your* pa . . . I always forget . . . *Rhys's* pa used to bring back such wonderful teas from foreign parts. Proper tea, from China, India, teas that smelled of perfume and sunshine . . . He was a sailor, you know, Rhodd, and he travelled the world.'

Her eyes glittered as she gazed into the fire. There was a shadow of trouble hanging about her that Rhodd had never sensed before. Rhodd could not see through the eyes of people in the same way as she could see through the eyes of animals, but she knew that Ma was looking far beyond the dark walls of the cottage. Seeing her lost husband, her lost son.

Cerys went on softly, 'The river ran wide and silver to the sea in those days, and the winds blew in fresh with every tide. Great ships came from all over the world and tied up at our quayside and there was fish enough and work enough for everyone.'

She sighed. 'And those bright boys who had a hunger for adventure, the boys who needed more than this dull place could offer . . .' She swallowed hard. 'They went to sea and travelled to exotic places and returned with their tall tales and their eyes shining with what they had seen.

That's what Rhys would have done, like his father, had he lived . . . if the river had not left us and taken all our hope with it.'

'What happened to him, Ma?' Rhodd asked.

There was a long pause. Cerys rarely spoke about her son and until now she'd always brushed off Rhodd's questions about him. She kept him well hidden in her heart. But whatever was troubling her, she seemed to have decided it was time for Rhodd to know more.

'I put him to bed one night, same as usual . . .' Ma shook her head hard as if it might shake away the memory. 'Not much older than you are now, he was. But always restless. This narrow village already felt too small for a boy like him.'

Rhodd thought about her friend Gar. He too was always restless, always talking about the world beyond the village – what wonders were done there, what *he* would do, if he only had the chance.

Ma was still talking, forcing herself to remember that terrible night. 'It was a full moon, and before I blew out Rhys's candle, we looked out at the marsh together.'

She still looks out at the marsh every night. Rhodd understood then something that had long puzzled her. *She's watching for Rhys to walk back home to her.* She could hardly bear to look at the sadness she recognised now in Ma's face.

She touched Ma's hand, but Ma hardly noticed. She was lost in longing for her son. 'Spring tide, it was, and the moonlight was shining silver on the full gullies. It was like a finger beckoning out to the sea.' She shivered and Red whined and patted her skirt with a consoling paw.

'I told him the old stories about his pa, sailing away down the river and into the world beyond with a gleam of adventure in his eyes . . . I don't know if that was what drew him out there. Perhaps it was my fault.' A pause. 'In the morning he was gone. Nobody had sight of him in the street, he was just gone. Later on, somebody said they might have seen something . . . something white out in the marsh. They thought maybe it might have been a boy's nightshirt, fluttering in the moonlight.'

Cerys sighed. 'Something called him, Rhodd, and he couldn't say no, not even for—'

His mother, she'd been going to say. But instead she stopped herself and shrugged. 'They never found a body. And he could swim, my Rhys – his pa made him learn . . .' A moment of remembered pride. 'But he never came back. All those flooded gutters, the shifting currents . . .' She shuddered. 'They reckoned he slipped, the mud must have dragged him down . . .' Her voice faded into silence.

Some dark thing swirled in Rhodd's mind and the scars on her legs ached like they hadn't ached since she was small. Something was stirring in her memory. But she didn't want to – wouldn't – look at it.

Late that night two small skinny figures slipped through the darkness and down the high street, towards the pub. Nobody was awake to see them creeping round the back towards the pig pen, nor to hear the careful sliding back of the bolt on the gate.

Two minutes later the Johnsons' prize pig was scampering away down the high street, urged on by whispers of encouragement.

'Go on, little chap!'

'Run for it, piggy!'

It wasn't the first time one of the Johnsons' pigs had mysteriously freed itself from its pen. This latest escapee joined a small herd of other pigs that had also somehow managed to undo that bolt and scarper away to snuffle up acorns in the woods above the village – to the endless mystification of Mrs Johnson. After all, how was she to know that the freeing of her pig always coincided with a particularly nasty bit of bullying by her sons?

The taste of revenge was sweet, and Rhodd and Gar sauntered home to their beds, sniggering in triumph.

CHAPTER 5

'Another boy gone, last night!'

Gar was waiting for Rhodd at the front of the school when she popped her head cautiously around the corner the next day. He was bursting with the news. 'Why-Why Jones, it was . . . his desk was empty this morning.'

The Johnson brothers' gang hadn't hung about to bully the pair of them today. They were already halfway along the street, heads down, subdued. Under orders to get home, on pain of punishment.

The shadow of a lost child had fallen on the village once more.

Rhodd nodded. She'd seen a crowd of villagers staring out at the marsh as she'd walked to meet Gar. They'd fallen silent and glared at her as she passed. Her back had prickled with their hostile stares but she'd grown used to that over the years. And she wasn't going to stop and ask questions.

'Why-Why . . .' Rhodd repeated the name. Even she knew Why-Why. She felt an unaccustomed pang of pity – she didn't often feel pity for anyone in this village. She had faced too much unkindness since she walked out of the wild – unkindness towards herself and her mother – to care much about any of them. But Why-Why had never done her any harm.

He was a pale, undergrown boy that nobody would look twice at in a crowd. Everyone called him Why-Why because he was always asking questions about the simplest stuff. Life had been a perpetual puzzle for Why-Why. He'd never been a bully, unlike most of the children of the village.

'What – just disappeared?' Rhodd asked.

Gar nodded. 'Full moon, it was, last night. Same as always. That's the second boy gone this spring. It's never been more than one a year – 'til now.'

Rhodd thought back to the moon shining in through her curtainless window the night before. She hadn't been able to sleep. She was always restless when the moon was full, but the last few moons had been worse. Even when she pulled her thin pillow over her head it was no help.

It was as if the rise and fall of the tides were tugging at her body, calling to something deep inside. Reminding her of the wild-ness within.

Gar and Rhodd set off down the street towards home. The women were still standing weeping on the quayside and the men were calling out on the edge of the marsh, 'Why-Why! Why-Why!' And amongst them his father's lone voice calling despairingly for 'Samuel' – the name he and Why-Why's mother had chosen with such pride for their firstborn son, seven short years before.

Why-Why's name echoed over the flat, brooding landscape and the gulls picked up the cry, wheeling up with it into the huge empty skies and then hurling it back to earth as if they were mocking the villagers below. 'Why-Why! Why-Why!'

But the line of searchers went no further than the first gully. Past that point, the sands shifted and the ditches moved with every tide, as slippery as the coils of a serpent. There was no safe path. And however much Why-Why was missed and mourned, no one dared venture further to find him. Not even his father. Not even his mother, staring out from the old quayside.

'What do you think happens to them, Rhodd?' Gar's voice was almost a whisper, as if he was afraid that something out there was listening and would hear the fear in his voice. He wasn't the only one. There was no child in the village that day who wasn't thinking that the next one to go could be them.

'Why are you asking me?' Rhodd snapped. She could still feel the accusing eyes of the crowd as if they were burning into her back. She was, quite suddenly, furious. Sick of the suspicion. 'You're like the rest of them – just because it's the marsh, you think I must know!'

Gar backed away. That cold flame was dancing in Rhodd's black eyes, pitiless, wild. But she had never turned it on him before. He was seeing something in Rhodd that scared him, a part of her that he could never know.

She didn't stop, even when she saw that look on his face. Her rage was relentless. 'Maybe *you* think it's my fault, like the rest of them do!' She sneered. 'Because that's where I came from, after all – the marsh – isn't it?' Her heart hammered with the anger boiling up inside her. 'Why don't you just say it? You blame me – it's my fault!' Rhodd was gasping for breath now. 'It's nothing to do with me!' she wailed. But she knew, even as she said it, that it was a lie.

'*Airk-Airk . . . airk-airk . . .*'

A savage cry rent the skies above and in an instant the

gulls stopped their mocking calls and scattered in terror. The Peregrine was over the marsh. Wings taut and sharp as arrowheads. Rhodd knew those eyes – which could detect the pollen dust on a bee's back and the quiver of a mouse's whiskers – would be able to tell her exactly what had happened to Why-Why. She knew instinctively that her falcon had seen the secret of what had befallen all those lost children. If only she dared to let him show her . . .

No! She snatched back her eyes to the earth. **I won't look!**

And her falcon wheeled away with a cry so harsh and furious it could have ripped out a hole from the sky. 'Airk-Airk . . . airk-airk . . .'

'I'm sorry, Rhodd.' Gar was watching her face, as cautious as if he was holding out a hand to a snarling dog. She said nothing, so he went on carefully, 'I only said that 'cos it's what everyone's asking. You know I don't think it's anything to do with you. How could it be anything to do with you?'

For the first time in their friendship, Rhodd knew that Gar was saying words that did not match up with the truth, did not match what he was really thinking. For the first time, he was looking at her with doubt in his face. But it was only a reflection of the doubt in her own face.

They walked on in silence. Silence wasn't the normal way of things for Rhodd and Gar. Something dark had slipped into the space between them. The sky was achingly empty. She realised she was wishing Gar would go away. Perhaps her falcon would come back if she was on her own. But at last Rhodd's savagery subsided a little.

'Sorry, Gar,' she said begrudgingly. 'But I honestly don't know any more than you.'

What she was saying was *almost* the truth. There was nothing that she actually *knew* about what had happened to Why-Why – except that the scars on her legs ached and the hairs on her neck were bristling like the hackles of a dog. And that deep memories were stirring, memories that she had for so long kept locked away.

Why will you not listen?

Why will you not look?

The danger grows out there.

You cannot keep yourself safe for ever.

CHAPTER 6

Gar was walking faster than normal and soon he drew ahead of Rhodd.

'I need to get home. Ma will be worried,' he called over his shoulder to her. But Rhodd didn't even try to catch up.

'Go on, then,' she muttered at Gar's departing back. She wanted to be on her own. She looked up at the sky. No falcon. *What if he doesn't come back?*

Fury and frustration – that's what she had heard in his cry as he'd wheeled away.

I won't look. That's what she'd told her falcon. Stubbornly holding on to her fear.

His cry was the voice of the wild-ness, the voice of the creatures of the air and earth, and there was accusation at the edge of it. It was an accusation of betrayal.

I'm sorry, she tried to tell him. **I have let you down.** But her mind-shapes floated up to an empty sky.

Rhodd gave a loose stone in her path a savage kick. It left a scrape on her bare toes. 'Ow!' Her eyes watered with the pain, but she kicked it again, harder. She wanted it to hurt. She deserved it.

In this brooding, angry mood, Rhodd's feet led her, despite her deep dread, to a place in the village she normally ran past with her eyes shut. It was a place that had given her nightmares since she was a small girl. But now she wanted to punish herself.

Beside the pub was a scruffy, unkempt patch of green where – in happier times – the whole village used to gather for May Day, to dance and sing and celebrate. But there was nothing to dance and sing about these days. The village was dying.

In the middle of the village green stood a wooden board. And even though she knew what would be there, the horror of seeing it once again stopped Rhodd in her tracks.

'No . . . no . . .' It made her cry out loud, just as it had on the day that she first saw it.

Nailed to the noticeboard were the broken bodies of dozens of tiny songbirds. Sparrows, linnets, finches, warblers – their little heads hanging limp and their feathers crushed where the nails had been driven in. And at the top, like their deposed king, hung the body of a great bird of prey.

It was a red kite and its russet feathers still glowed like the embers of a fire, its mighty talons dangling. So much power, now useless in death. Once the proud hunter, now the prey of small boys.

Rhodd couldn't read the words on the notice pinned up above those pathetic corpses but Gar had told her what it said.

Sparrows and small birds: three pence
per dozen dead.
Birds of prey: four pence
per each one dead.

It was the gamekeeper that worked for the local landowner, Lord Stanley, who paid out that blood money to the boys. The gamekeeper called the birds 'vermin' – he claimed the small ones damaged the crops and the hawks killed the livestock.

So much senseless suffering. So much song silenced. So much wild beauty, crushed. Rhodd knew who those boys were. Cowards armed with slingshots who killed for a few pennies of pocket money. The same boys who made her life and Gar's life a misery.

Any softness or pity for the villagers that Rhodd had ever felt cooled and hardened into a blade of steel. A blade which – in that savage moment – she would happily have used to cut out all their hearts.

For years, Rhodd had used her trick of shifting inside another creature's head to keep her company in her loneliness. Sometimes she had used it to keep herself safe. But now, for the first time, she longed to use her gift to get vengeance. Vengeance for the wild world that truly owned her heart.

Rhodd hissed, 'I wish there really was some savage beast out there on the marsh. I would bend its fury to my will and I would bid it swallow this village whole.'

That evening, just one slight figure slipped through the moon shadows and down the high street. Rhodd hadn't woken Gar tonight. This vengeance belonged to her alone.

The boys who had earned the blood money with their slingshots were woken from their dreams, one after the other, by a soft knocking at their window.

When they looked out, the small ghostly shape of a child in a white nightshirt was standing there in the darkness, staring in at them with black, hollow eyes.

In their terror, it might have been Why-Why, or any of the other children lost to the marsh. For a few long, spine-chilling minutes, the child looked at them in silence. And then it pointed and beckoned to them and mouthed, soundless, through the glass, 'You will be next.'

That was the last time any of those boys slept sound in their beds, without fear.

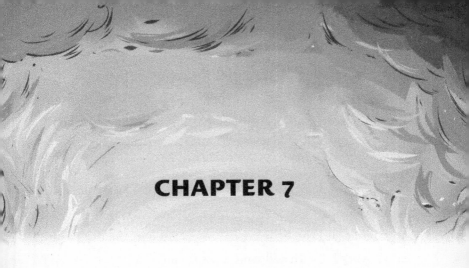

CHAPTER 7

Spring passed, a sultry, sulking spring, and the hottest in living memory. Green shoots faded fast to yellow and withered in the dry earth. Nothing thrived.

One morning Rhodd stepped out of the door and jumped back in horror as her bare toes nudged at a soft heap of feathers. Her heart, for a second, stopped beating.

She bent quickly to scoop up the body in her hands and breathed out a sob that was as much relief as pity. Her heart beat again. It was not her falcon. She held the limp bundle close. It weighed nothing, a pathetic bundle of bones beneath feathers. It was a starling, the brilliance of his plumage dulled in death.

Oh, my darling . . .

She knew that starling. Such a cocky little chap he had

been, swaggering about in all his rainbow finery before taking to the air with the rest of his flock to form a murmuration that had filled the skies with a whirling, soaring exuberance. All that joy was over for him now.

Red!

She turned to the dog to share her pain, but he just looked away.

Rhodd laid the little corpse in a scrape in the dry earth and covered it with soil, and went to find Gar.

'Happening all over.' Gar shrugged when she told him. He looked as bewildered as she was. 'Birds falling from the sky, stone dead. Like they've been breathing poisoned air.'

After that Rhodd held her breath when she stepped out of the house every morning until she glimpsed her falcon. She spent her days with her eyes fixed on the relentlessly blue skies, watching him. He wheeled higher in the sky these days, as if he was holding himself apart from her. But at least he was back, still watching over her.

Not you, not you. I could not live without you.

But as the dry weeks passed into summer, it wasn't just the birds that were dying. A sickness crept into the village, and a line of new grey headstones sprang up in the churchyard. And with it, a growing unease.

'It ain't natural,' went the murmurs. Tempers grew

short. One day after school, when Rhodd and Gar were running past the pub as usual, she'd heard the guttural gathering of phlegm in someone's throat. A gobbet of spittle just missed her bare foot.

Someone muttered. 'Nothing but bad luck in this village since we took that creature in.'

After that, Ma wouldn't let Rhodd go with Gar to listen to lessons outside the schoolroom. 'I don't want you going down there any more,' she said. 'It wouldn't take much for them to turn on you, in this mood.'

So Rhodd stayed close to home and her alphabet book lay untouched, gathering dust on the table. She felt safer from the villagers inside those thick stone walls and she fought down her old terror of being stifled indoors. Because when she couldn't see the wide skies and smell the dark earth, the exhausting restlessness and rage that had been stirring inside her was stilled. It was easier to forget the wild world when she was in the dark cottage, close to Ma.

Here was peace at least. Peace from struggling to navigate this world that she had stumbled into, out of the wild. Peace from the question that rattled endlessly through her thoughts when she was alone. *Why am I here?*

But in her head her own voice was also whispering, *Coward.*

I need to help Ma, she told herself and she stuffed her ears against that accusing voice. *She needs me.* But her thoughts still whispered incessantly, *Coward, coward . . .* And high above the roof of the dark cottage, she knew without seeing that her falcon was circling and calling to her, '*Airk, airk.*' She did not want to hear the growing anger and accusation in that cry.

It was true, though, that Ma always seemed tired these days, and it did mean more chores for Rhodd. She had never really seen the point of most of the chores Ma insisted on. Why brush up loose soil from a floor that was made of earth? And why move dust from inside the cottage to outside the cottage when the wind would soon blow it back inside again anyway?

But one thing Rhodd had always flat-out refused to do was to disturb the spiders from their webs. The first time Ma had asked her to sweep the corners of the ceiling, Rhodd saw through the spiders' tiny accusing eyes and heard their furious scolding as the cobweb brush swooped towards them to destroy their carefully crafted webs. After that she'd have nothing more to do with it. 'They don't like it,' was the only explanation she could give to Ma.

She also had a long-term arrangement with a family of mice under her bed, who had agreed not to make too much noise or mess in exchange for occasional crumbs of goat's cheese. Cerys pretended not to know. Housework was one of the few things she had been forced to compromise over.

It was the hottest afternoon so far and Rhodd was brushing the floor and listening to the spiders whilst they sang their scratchy rhythmic web-weaving songs, when a knock came at the door.

Ma did not stir from her chair. 'See who that is, Rhodd.' It wasn't like her not to be busy, out tending the vegetable patch they depended on for food or milking the goat or making bread or . . . there was always a long list of jobs to be done. But today it seemed she wasn't doing any of them.

Rhodd went to the door. A buxom red-faced woman stood sweating in the sunshine. A quick flicker of worry crossed Rhodd's face as she recognised the Johnson boys' mother. Why was she here? Had her sons talked about that ghostly apparition at their window?

Ma Johnson took a step back when she saw Rhodd at the door and her little eyes narrowed. Rhodd knew she had always had her suspicions about who kept freeing her pigs. But then the woman did something surprising. She made a quick, furtive gesture with her hand that Rhodd had never seen before. Like she was warding off something bad.

Cerys stepped up quickly beside Rhodd and pushed her protectively behind her. She'd seen the gesture, and she knew it was directed at her daughter. And unlike Rhodd, she knew what it meant. It was the sign against witch-evil.

Rhodd glanced up at her mother's face. It was very white, but her lips were clamped tight in an angry red line between her teeth. She looked like she was trying to stop something from escaping out of her mouth.

'What do you want, Mary-Ann?' Rhodd had never heard Ma speak to anyone so angrily. She was normally very careful to be polite. But it wasn't just anger she could smell on Ma. There was fear too.

'My husband's sick,' replied Ma Johnson. 'Do you . . . do you have summat you can give him?'

Rhodd wasn't very good at human faces. Was that fear in Ma Johnson's face too?

'What ails him?' Ma let out the words like bubbles escaping from a lid clamped tight on a boiling saucepan.

'A fever . . . aches . . . sweating . . . Same as—'

'Same as what carried off Six-Foot Smith last week,' Ma interrupted, merciless. 'He was a strong man, Six-Foot Smith.'

Ma Johnson paled and nodded. 'Can you . . .'

Cerys glared at the woman in front of her. Since she'd

got married and come to live here in the village, she'd never liked Mary-Ann Johnson, nor her bully of a husband. And she knew from the bruises Rhodd brought home that their three sons were growing up to be bullies just like their father.

'Please, Cerys . . .'

Cerys was well aware that the villagers only stopped short of calling her 'witch' because she'd always been useful to them, because she knew what herbs could help most common ailments. After she lost her husband, they'd made it obvious they didn't want Cerys living too close, with her uncanny skills. That's when she'd come to live in this tumbledown cottage on the edge-lands, closest to the marsh.

She'd always feared it wouldn't take much for them to turn against her and her wild child. It seemed that time was coming.

But Ma Johnson was begging her. And Cerys knew what it was to lose a husband.

'I have something that should bring down the fever,' she said slowly. 'But I warn you, it may not be enough. The Sickness does not give up easily once it has someone in its grip. Some it takes quickly; some it takes slowly. But Six-Foot wasn't the first.' She added under her breath, as she turned inside to find the herbs, 'And I fear he won't be the last.'

Ma Johnson watched Cerys's face closely as she paid over her penny in exchange for the twist of dried herbs.

'What is it, then, this Sickness?' she demanded quickly. 'Folks don't get sick in the spring, 'tis winter fevers that carry people off . . . It ain't normal . . . just like this heat ain't normal neither.'

The suspicion was dark in her eyes, and she peered round Cerys to seek out Rhodd in the shadows. Looking for someone to blame.

'I don't know. I told you, I've not seen this Sickness before.' Cerys was already closing the door. 'And I'm warning you, the herbs may not work.'

Mrs Johnson was bolder now that she'd got the medicine she'd come for. 'It's a curse, come from the marsh,' she hissed at Cerys. 'She brought it with—'

Ma slammed the door in the woman's face. But they could still hear her shouting from the street.

'We should never have let you take that creature in!'

CHAPTER 8

After Ma Johnson had gone, there was silence. Rhodd twitched the broom unnecessarily around the room for the sake of keeping busy, but her eyes kept returning to Ma who was sitting in front of the fire, still shivering in spite of the summer heat.

'Bring me a handful of those hazelnuts, Rhodd,' Ma said at last.

Rhodd tipped a handful of nuts from their pot and handed them to her mother. 'It's the last, Ma,' she told her. But it was more to try and draw Cerys's eyes away from the flames than to tell her anything she didn't know. She knew what Ma wanted them for. It must be important to sacrifice their last few hazelnuts.

'There are things I need to know, child.'

As Rhodd watched, Cerys grew still. She gathered stillness about her, as if she were weaving a web every bit as fine as the spiders', yet a thousand times more secret. This was the work of another world and if the villagers had seen her now, they would indeed have called her 'witch'. Rhodd was the only one who had seen this, and even she had seen it rarely.

Ma was asking questions forbidden to ordinary mortals. Questions about what was to come.

With a quick motion, timed in answer to a call that Rhodd could not hear, Ma tossed the hazelnuts into the flames.

They flared up, orange then blue then green and a rainbow of colours that changed too fast to tell. Ma's eyes never flinched from the blaze.

Rhodd whispered, 'What do you see, Ma?'

What Cerys saw shifted the expressions on her face like dark clouds scudding across the sun.

'Death,' she whispered. 'Death.' She was shivering so hard that Rhodd had to wrap her arms around Ma to hold her in the chair. In spite of her fear of fire, Rhodd forced herself to look. But she could not see what Cerys saw.

'A journey . . .' Ma clutched at Rhodd's arms as if to

bind her tight. And then her whole body stiffened, limbs gripped by something she could not control.

'*Earth will be swept away by Water* . . .

Water will quench Fire . . .

Fire will consume Air . . .

Air will rise into Spirit . . .'

Cerys the Wise Woman was chanting and shaking. Pain was etched on her face as if it was being carved by the tip of a knife. 'No! Not again!'

And then there was a change. Ma had been shown something new. Her rigid body softened and her green eyes filled with wonder.

'How can that be?' What she was seeing Rhodd could not tell.

The flames died back as fast as they had flared up. Ma stood quickly and raked up the embers. She said nothing about what she had seen. And Rhodd knew better than to ask.

But there was something in her mother's face that Rhodd had not seen for a long time. Was it joy, perhaps?

CHAPTER 9

'I need you to go and get more of those herbs this evening, Rhodd. The Johnsons won't be the only ones to come knocking at the door. I reckon this Sickness is here to stay.'

Ma's face was set grim next morning, over their scant breakfast. She said nothing of her conjured visions of the night before. The brief joy was gone, replaced by shadows that looked more like fear.

Cerys was paler than Rhodd had ever seen her; her eyes gleamed like fresh grass beneath melting snow. But it wasn't just how white she looked that shocked Rhodd. Ma had never before asked her to go and pick herbs. She'd never even risked taking Rhodd with her. 'Don't need to give that lot more cause to gossip about you,' she'd always said. 'It would take little enough for them to witch-call you.' Why would she make Rhodd take that risk now? For a brief moment, Rhodd felt like that fledgling being pushed from its branch.

As if she had sensed Rhodd's doubt, Cerys reached out to lay her palm flat against her cheek.

'I know I've never asked you to go before, Rhodd, but they can't think any worse of us than they do now,' she said gently. 'Maybe if they see you helping me with the medicine – and maybe if it works – they might not turn against you.' She shrugged. 'If we can stop the Sickness taking hold it might stop the witch-calling.' She made it sound like a big 'if'.

Red came and pushed his cold nose into Ma's hand as she sank on to her chair. Rhodd knew Red could smell the fear on Ma just like she could. She also knew that it was a life-and-death matter to be branded a witch in these superstitious times. It was cause enough for a girl to be put on trial for her life – if they even bothered with a trial. In a village like this, shut off from the world, they'd settle matters themselves sooner than bring in outsiders to pry on their affairs. They'd always made their own rough justice in this place.

But it wasn't only fear that Rhodd could smell on her mother. There was something else.

No! Rhodd shook her head and turned away when Red tried to tell her what he knew. She refused to see Ma through his eyes. She didn't want to know. But not talking to Red just added to the silence that was growing around her as the birdsong still faded from the skies. Silence that was shattered only by the angry '*airk-airk*' of the Peregrine circling and calling to her inside the cottage.

Cerys pointed to a jar to show Rhodd which herbs she needed. 'They grow just below the sea wall. At the bottom of the steps by the marsh.'

Rhodd backed away. 'No, Ma!' Terror flared deep in her black eyes. 'I can't go there!'

'You won't have to go on to the marsh,' Cerys reassured her. 'The plants grow close to the wall, where the river used to flow. The banks were always green with herbs in those days,' she added wistfully.

She was watching Rhodd's face intently. She could see the fear there. But she could not know that Rhodd was harkening to the impatient, furious wing-beats of her hovering falcon above the roof.

There was so much that still puzzled Ma about her wild daughter's curious contradiction between raw courage and gut-deep fear. Rhodd had always refused even to look at the marsh – the marsh that she had walked out of all those years before. What had happened to her there? What had she been fleeing? And what secrets did she hold so close that she would not share them, not even with Cerys?

Cerys was a Wise Woman, and did not normally hold with the ignorant, superstitious fears of the villagers. But she had always known that there was indeed a darkness out on the marsh that was to be feared. And the time was coming that it would have to be faced.

She pulled her daughter close. 'Courage, Rhodd!' It was what she'd said years before when she first held that quivering ball of animal instinct in her arms. 'It's time to find your courage.'

And then she added, 'Take Gar with you. You and Gar will keep each other safe.'

But to Rhodd it sounded like she said it more in hope than because she actually believed it.

CHAPTER 10

Dusk was falling as Rhodd and Gar set off. There was an oppressive heat hanging in the air. A storm was brewing. Rhodd tried not to look at the ominous crimson sunset glowering over the marsh. It looked too much like fire.

Bethan had agreed to Gar going with Rhodd only if he swore not to set a foot further than the bottom step down from the sea wall. 'Like she thinks some monster will jump out and grab me if I step on a bit of mud,' Gar scoffed. Then a barn owl hissed suddenly out of the shadows and he jumped and clutched at Rhodd's arm.

They both laughed, but the laughter didn't convince either of them. They set a fast pace, speeding up even more as they passed the hostile staring eyes outside the pub.

'Come on,' urged Gar. 'They're watching.' Rhodd

didn't need any urging after being spat at the last time.

Only when they were well past the pub did they feel safe enough to slow to a walk. The steps towards which they were heading lay on the stretch of sea wall on the other side of the schoolhouse, at the far end of the village, and it was quieter, almost deserted here. Very few children were left to play out these days once dusk gathered and darkness rolled in from the marsh.

Rhodd glanced up. **There you are!**

She had never seen her falcon hover so low. She could clearly make out the yellow rims bright about his eyes, the droop of his dark moustache that gave him such a look of fierce melancholy. In all his years watching over her, he had never come close enough to touch. Her heart had always ached to hold him, but she knew it was like yearning to hug the wind or wrap her arms around a cloud. He was a creature of the air, not the earth. He wasn't hers to hold.

There was an urgency about the furious beating of his wings this evening. And his cry had become a shriek of desperate warning. '*Airk, airk, airk!*'

What is it? she asked him. She could tell he was deeply troubled, uneasy – and angry. Cocooned inside the cottage, keeping herself safe, she had hardly seen him over the last weeks. But she had felt his impatience growing, even as she had tried to ignore it. He hung there above her head and that mournful, savage shriek came again. '*Airk, airk, airk!*'

You must look, child. Now! Now! Now! It is time.

His gaze was fixed on the marsh, where the sunset was firing the ditches with flame. She knew he wanted her to see what he saw, but she was resisting with all her might. It had become a struggle between them and it was agony for Rhodd to push away the wild spirit that was part of her own soul.

No, no, I cannot! I am not ready . . .

You must look. Before it is too late!

The thread between them tensed and jangled like the overtightened string of a violin . . . as if it might at any moment break . . .

Look, look!

No! I cannot!

Once again Rhodd snatched back her gaze before she could see what he saw.

I do not want to know.

'*Airk, airk, airk!*'

With a final despairing cry her falcon wheeled and soared away, black eyes flaring with fire. In moments he was a dot in the reddening sky, hundreds of feet above the earth. And then he was gone.

It was as if he had found a rent in the air and slipped into another world where she could not follow.

Rhodd let out a cry of loss that was wrenched from the depths of her wild heart. She had never felt so lonely, so bereft. The thread between her and her falcon had broken.

You have kept your eyes closed for too long.

You are forgetting your wild-ness within.

You are forsaking the wild-ness without.

I cannot help you more.

CHAPTER 11

Rhodd walked on with her eyes fixed to the ground. She was trying not to think about the finality of that last cry. She could not look up. This was a pain she could never share with Gar. She had never even told Ma about her falcon, whatever she might have guessed.

You are angry with me. Why are you so angry? she asked.

It was the voice of a small, frightened child. And – listening to herself – Rhodd suddenly understood her falcon's anger. She realised she could no longer pretend to be that child – the child she had been when she walked out of the marsh.

It was time.

Gar was watching Rhodd. He had seen something pass

between his friend and the falcon and he had heard the cry she had let out. He recognised the desolation in her face even if he couldn't understand what had happened.

'What is it, that thing you do?' he asked. He was trying to sound casual.

'What thing?' Rhodd's reply flashed fierce and sharp as a talon.

Gar refused to flinch. He had decided he wasn't going to let himself be scared of Rhodd after the last time. 'You know, when you . . . talk to creatures.'

'I don't . . . *talk* . . .' A sneer. And the edge of a growl. She had never spoken about this. Not even to Ma.

'What, then?' Gar persisted. He liked to know how things worked. 'Go on, tell me, Rhodd.'

Rhodd swallowed the growl. Remembered that this was Gar and they'd tumbled together through childhood like wolf cubs. She could not lose this friendship. Especially now beneath the empty sky. Gar was all she had left, him and Ma.

'I see . . . what they see . . . I see with their eyes,' she told him reluctantly. It sounded like such a small thing. When really it was everything.

'That's amazing! Almost as good as . . .' Gar's eyes were shining with wonder. Even if this wasn't something man-made. '. . . as good as electricity!'

Rhodd had no idea what electricity was – apart from knowing it was Gar's latest obsession. He was always telling her about new inventions and experiments the schoolmaster had shown him in his books. Amazing things people were doing in the wide world outside this narrow village.

His enthusiasm encouraged her to risk telling him a little more. 'I hear things they hear . . .'

'But you can't *talk* to them?' Gar asked. He looked disappointed, and Rhodd bristled like an offended cat.

'We don't *talk*,' she sneered. 'I just . . .' As ever, human language was falling short of what she needed. There weren't words for this. 'I just *know*. And they *know*.'

Gar nodded. He seemed satisfied. He thought for a bit. 'Will they do anything you want, Rhodd? Like little tricks and stuff?' His eyes were round and shiny as silver pennies. 'That would be *really* amazing!'

Rhodd snarled at him, her face a mask of fury. 'Do I *control* them, you mean?'

Gar stepped quickly back. Even to him she was terrifying when she looked like that. A savage thing. 'No, I didn't mean—'

'Make them do what I *want*?' she interrupted him.

'They aren't my *toys*, you numbskull! We are made of the same stuff, made of the same earth and the same water and the same air . . . the same . . .'

She paused, groping for a word for the element that flickered inside her heart. What was it? 'Fire . . .' she finished doubtfully.

Rhodd was shaking. Even the word 'fire' scared her, but it was the only one that came close. 'They are part of me and I am part of them,' she finished. 'How could I ever *dare* to make them do my bidding? I wouldn't even *want* to . . .'

But then she realised that wasn't true. Another lie, another half-truth. She remembered the fury with which she had longed to unleash some mighty beast on the village to avenge those pathetic little birds, just a few weeks before. But she did not like it.

She glanced at Gar. She hated herself now for lashing out. There was real fear in his face and the truth was that she had scared herself. Was scared *of* herself.

It was a glimpse of something dark, deep in her soul. She did not understand it. She shivered. Could she ever control it?

CHAPTER 12

It wasn't until they reached the end of the village that Rhodd – who'd been storming ahead swinging Ma's herb basket like a weapon – stopped shaking enough to talk.

'Sorry,' she muttered.

'Sorry too,' said Gar. 'I didn't understand.' It felt like the pair of them were doing a lot of sorry-saying these days. Like they were having to learn each other all over again. But then he added cheerfully, 'Still don't, really.'

Rhodd's mouth split into something that was trying to be a grin but ended as a grimace. The ominous, glowering dusk was pressing on her like a weight.

'I don't think I do either, Gar,' she confessed. She was only just starting to accept that her gift of communicating with creatures had not been given to her just for her own entertainment, like some special birthday present to comfort a lost and lonely child. There was a deeper reason for it. But she still didn't really know what that reason was.

'We need to go down there.' She set off down the steps from the quayside. It was a relief to stop talking.

The windows of the closest cottages were blazing red, blinded by the reflected sunset. It was impossible to tell who might be watching. Stepping on to the marsh was breaking an unwritten law in the village. It felt wrong.

A low growl shook the thick, storm-threatening air. It sounded like a warning from something brooding out in there in the wild-ness. Something lurking there, waiting to lure them away along with the other lost children.

'Thunder,' Gar said, dismissing it. 'It was just thunder.' But neither of them was really sure.

He followed Rhodd slowly down the steps. She was keeping her eyes firmly on her feet, trying to concentrate on the sandstone beneath her bare soles. It felt as warm as if it had been quarried from summer sunshine. But at the bottom she stopped dead. Gar bumped into her back, almost sending her toppling into the mud.

'Gar,' she whispered. 'There's nothing here. It's all dead.'

Ma had reassured her that last time she'd come here

looking for herbs, there had been plenty of fresh green growth. Now there was nothing but scorched brown leaves.

Gar nodded. 'Almost like it's been burned.'

Rhodd searched with her eyes, all the way along the bottom of the sea wall. As far as she could see, there was nothing left alive, like it had been poisoned.

'It's all gone, Gar.' She felt sick. What she was seeing felt so bitterly wrong. 'It's supposed to be summer. Stuff should be growing.'

'Why are we whispering?' whispered Gar.

Rhodd paused, listened. 'Because it is too quiet.'

Gar considered and then nodded. Since that low growl, a silence had hung over the marsh that neither of them had ever heard before. No birds were calling and nothing stirred. Nothing but a restless, unsettling whisper from the wind in the reeds.

'Look, Rhodd.'

Rhodd cautiously raised her eyes to Gar's face to see where he was looking. So far, she had kept her eyes locked on the muddy ground close to the sea wall. But Gar was staring out at the reeds and she took a deep breath and forced herself to follow his eyes.

'The reeds are dying too.' Gar was still whispering.

He was right. The reeds were the colour of winter,

grey as gravestones. The smell of decay hung about them. They were rotting in the water that was supposed to give them life.

Rhodd leaned back against the sandstone wall, in need of something to hold her upright. She felt hollow, emptied out. All she could sense here was anger, rolling in great waves off the marsh. Where – or what – was it coming from?

It had taken her until now to realise the most devastating thing of all. She wasn't able to see through a single creature's eyes, couldn't hear through any creature's ears. She could barely even breathe. If there was anything left alive here, it had turned its back on her.

She looked up, desperate to see her falcon, desperate for his comfort. But he was nowhere to be seen. The blazing sunset sky was empty. She felt a sudden terror that the thread between them could never now be mended. Had he abandoned her for ever?

Rhodd's knees buckled beneath her and she sank on to the foul mud, with a wail that echoed out into the wild marsh. But no answering cries came from that place. And at that moment she knew. She had refused to listen for too long.

'Rhodd!' Gar kneeled beside her. 'What is it?'

'I . . . don't . . . know.' It had never been harder to find words. 'But I have . . . to . . . find . . . out. It's my . . . fault.' Rhodd was gasping.

'How can it be your fault?' But Gar sounded no more certain of anything than Rhodd. This was beyond any human explaining.

As the pair of them huddled together at the edge of the dead marsh, a faint mew sounded from the reeds.

Rhodd's head lifted, ears pricked, alert.

A sluggish stream of bubbles was moving across the surface of the dark, putrid ditch. A pair of nostrils snuffled above the muddy water . . . a soft gasp for air.

'Otter,' breathed Rhodd. The lithe, supple body rippled closer. A pair of dark eyes rose above the whiskered muzzle and glared at her. There was an accusation in that glare. It was an accusation of betrayal. She knew that otters rejoiced in water just as her falcon rejoiced in the wind. But this creature had none of that joy.

She waited, reaching out to it with all her senses, groping to see with its eyes, hear with its ears. How could she live if all the creatures of the earth deserted her?

Please . . . tell me. I am listening . . .

The otter hauled itself out. Slowly, so slowly. Beads of water ran from its thick coat. They were crimsoned by the sunset and they looked for a moment like drops of blood.

Rhodd saw with its eyes. But there was nothing in its mind-shapes but desolation and despair.

You turned your back on us. The otter's anger swirled around her head.

'Oh . . .' A cry of agony escaped from her gut. It was the same pain she had felt when her Peregrine had wheeled away and left her.

She crawled on her knees through the mud to the otter, kneeled next to it. Two pups were clinging to their mother's body like a life raft. So new to the world that their eyes were still closed . . . all grey softness but for the pink yawn of their mewling mouths.

You must save them. I cannot. The otter nosed her babies gently from her back. **It is up to you now,** she told Rhodd. **You have to come back and fight for us. It is time.**

And the otter slipped back into the darkening marsh and was gone, leaving her pups behind, blind and weeping for their mother.

Rhodd cupped the helpless otter pups in her hands and Gar reached out to stroke the smooth fur. Rhodd tried to break through their blind panic to console them but they were too little to understand anything but their loss. The cubs nuzzled at her fingers, seeking in vain for their mother's comfort.

Hush, hush . . . you're safe now. Safe with me.

The lie – for she had not the faintest idea how to do their mother's bidding – did nothing to quiet their mewling. Only when she tucked them tight against her warm body, under her smock, did their cries quieten.

It is up to you now. The otter's stern rebuke was echoing around her head.

'Ma will know what to do with them.' Rhodd stood up, knees black with mud.

Gar was blinking hard, head ducked, trying not to let Rhodd see his wet face. He had not understood everything, but he had understood enough.

He picked up the empty basket so Rhodd could keep her arms around the pups, and together they trailed back up the steps from the marsh. The crimson sun had almost dipped below the horizon but it was still flaming like the head of an angry god.

Every time Rhodd glanced back, her own black shadow was following her, a long accusing finger.

You turned your back on us.

That night Rhodd lay staring into darkness. Sleep would not come.

Flashes of lightning ripped great gashes out of the sky beyond her curtainless window and the crack and crash of the breaking storm shook the earth. An anger had been unleashed in the wild. The doors of the cottage were shaking and the roof groaned with the onslaught of the rain. The scars on Rhodd's legs burned like they had never burned before.

She could hear the otter pups whimpering in their sleep. Ma had warmed some goat's milk and they had licked it from Rhodd's fingers until they fell asleep between Red's paws. Just as Rhodd herself had once done, when she first crept out of the wild.

Was it some great beast out there, raging because the otter pups had been snatched from its grasp? Or was it the natural world rising up in anger against Rhodd because she had refused to listen for so long?

A nameless and shapeless dread hung over her. The task facing her felt immense, overwhelming. If the creatures that had spoken to her all her life turned their backs on her – if her falcon did not return – who was there to tell her what she must do?

CHAPTER 13

The tolling of the church bell woke Rhodd next morning, but it wasn't Sunday.

'The Lord is coming! The Lord's on his way!'

There were shouts from the street and a great banging on the door of Gar and Bethan's cottage . . . then running feet and the same urgent knocking on Rhodd's own door, the same shouts. 'The Lord is coming! The Lord is on his way!'

Rhodd and Ma had gone to church every Sunday until the last few weeks, when the hisses and hostile whispers made it clear they were not welcome. Before that, Cerys had always insisted on them going, said it might stop the villagers from gossiping about them both. So Rhodd had heard plenty of sermons in her life. Enough to wonder –

when somebody shouted that the Lord was coming – whether this was the end of the world?

She swung her legs out of the bed and ran to the back door. 'What's happening, Ma?'

Ma was outside milking the goat. She took one look at Rhodd's scared face and laughed. It was good to hear Ma laugh. She didn't laugh very often nowadays, not that great generous belly-laugh that Rhodd had always loved.

'Don't worry, Rhodd, it's only that pompous fool Lord Stanley calling a meeting. Just because he owns the village and all the land round here, he thinks we have to jump whenever he says "jump". He'll want everyone to be there to hear what he's got to say. We'd best get ready and go and see what's happening.'

She carried the milk pail inside and poured a little for Rhodd to give to the otter pups. 'But I don't reckon it'll be good news for any of us,' she added. 'He never comes here these days, not now the village makes no money for him.'

Rhodd crouched down to feed the pups who were whimpering between Red's paws. The old dog gave them a lick with his great pink tongue and that quietened them. He would not look at Rhodd. There was still a terrible silence between them.

The air was fresher after the storm, but clouds hung

heavy over the village. Ma and Rhodd met Bethan and Gar outside their cottage and they joined the long line of subdued villagers heading towards the pub. Rhodd kept glancing anxiously up at the falconless sky. It was like losing sight of her soul. Her falcon was what tethered her to the wild.

They joined the crowd waiting on the village green, keeping themselves to the back so as not to attract attention. Rhodd kept her face turned away from the bird-catchers' board. She couldn't trust herself to look at it again, for fear that her bloodlust for vengeance would return and this time it would be beyond her controlling.

Nobody seemed to have any notion what the meeting was about and wild rumours were being bandied about.

'Nitwits,' Cerys muttered in contempt. 'These numbskulls know no more than we do.'

'Jim Johnson died last night,' Rhodd heard somebody saying. Ma Johnson was standing red-eyed with grief at the front of the crowd, surrounded by her sons.

Heads turned to stare at Cerys. Everyone knew that Ma Johnson had gone to Cerys for help. And everyone knew her herbs had failed to save him.

'He was the seventh,' someone whispered.

Rhodd could feel anger swirling like black smoke

through the crowd. It wouldn't take much to whip it up into flames.

At last there came a rattle of wheels and the clatter of horses' hooves.

'It's His Lordship,' went the word as a smartly turned-out open carriage appeared round the corner. It was a brilliant yellow and it was pulled by two matching grey horses, their heads forced fashionably – and painfully – high.

Rhodd winced as she briefly saw through the horses' blinkered eyes and felt their half-blind, barely suppressed panic at not being able to see what was around them. She felt what they felt, the harness weighing heavy on her own neck, and the metal biting into her own tongue.

It is all right, she tried to soothe them.

She shook her head free from the horses' pain, tried to focus on what the people around her were saying, tried to understand the human stuff that was going on.

A gentleman dressed entirely and very expensively in black climbed down from the carriage. 'Hold the horses,' he barked at the groom. 'I don't want anybody touching my new carriage. Paint's barely dry.'

'His Lordship!' someone whispered. 'Now we'll know what's what . . .'

'Classy turn-out that is, must 'ave cost a pretty penny.'

Lord Stanley barked at a footman. 'Nail that notice to the front of the public house, where they can all see it.' The footman, wearing the same dark green livery as the groom, jumped down from the carriage with a roll of paper.

The men tipped their caps and the women bobbed their curtsies as Lord Stanley strutted towards the crowd. All but Ma and Bethan. They didn't curtsey or bow their heads. Rhodd thought the pair of them were staring at the man as if they had knives in their eyes.

'Lord Stanley.' The muttered name twisted Ma's mouth like a bad taste. Rhodd had never seen such contempt in her face.

Bethan glared at His Lordship and tried to pull Gar close to her skirts. But Gar wriggled free. 'Let me see,' he protested.

He was the only one watching the footman as he unrolled the paper and hammered it up over the pub noticeboard. And he was the only one who bothered to read the words written on it.

'Land for sale,' Gar whispered but nobody heard him. They were all watching Lord Stanley, waiting to be told what he had to say.

His Lordship's head rose like a solid column of rubbery

flesh from his neck, as smooth and flat as if it had been made from whale skin. The smoothness was barely interrupted by the tiniest eyes and mouth Rhodd had ever seen, but his nose rose from his face like a great beak.

A gaggle of crows were looking on, curious – as crows always seemed to be – about the fuss. Rhodd suppressed a giggle as one of the crows stuck its own beak in the air and started strutting along the old quayside wall, legs straight, its wings pinned tight against its body like a close-fitting tail coat. Just like Lord Stanley.

She'd always known that crows had a sense of humour and she knew exactly what this one was up to. She'd watched it mimicking people before, for the sheer fun of it. Another couple of other crows were cawing with laughter – one was laughing so hard it lost its balance and tumbled off the wall before righting itself and flapping off, embarrassed.

Rhodd laughed out loud but Gar nudged her to shut up. Nobody else was laughing.

Lord Stanley hadn't noticed the crows any more than he had noticed the bobbing and scraping from the villagers. He didn't bother to introduce himself.

'None of you has paid me a penny in rent for the last year,' he said. Not a single expression or emotion shook his face. 'I am going to pull down these houses and sell off the land. This village is no longer necessary.'

A confused mutter started up.

'But we ain't got no money to pay rent,' one brave voice protested.

'We can't fish . . .'

'There's no work . . .'

Lord Stanley ignored them. 'I am not a charity. The land may have some value, but no buyer will want the houses. The village is worthless to anybody without the river. And the river—' He paused as if there was something he knew but wasn't saying. 'For some reason beyond our understanding, the river is gone. Nature moves in mysterious ways.'

In his face something slithered beneath the smooth skin. It looked like an eel hiding itself beneath water weeds. Rhodd smelled a lie. But what could this man be lying about?

Then Lord Stanley delivered the final blow. 'I want you all out of your homes – and the village empty – by the end of the month. The houses will be pulled down the following day.'

CHAPTER 14

A wail went up from one of the women. There was a collective gasp, angry shouts from the crowd.

'But that's less than two weeks!'

'Lived here for centuries, my family has . . .'

'This is our home . . .'

'Where will we go?'

Rhodd looked round, confused. If she ever thought about it at all, she saw the home she shared with Ma as a rabbit saw its warren, as a bird saw its nest. Not as something that could be taken away, not as something that could be sold.

But nobody dared to challenge His Lordship's right to sell the village. His word was the only law they knew.

Lord Stanley was being careful not to look at anybody

directly. But Rhodd noticed his eyes hesitate for a moment over Bethan and Gar with what might have been a faint flicker of interest, before looking away quickly. Those eyes . . . where had she seen eyes that blue before?

'What about school?' Gar pushed himself forward before Bethan could stop him. Lord Stanley was already turning towards his carriage but Gar grabbed his perfectly tailored black sleeve and held him back. 'What about our lessons?'

A couple of boys sniggered. Gar was the only one in the village who cared about school.

Lord Stanley stared at Gar's hand on his arm as if in disbelief that any of these villagers should dare to touch him. He looked up at the clever, delicately boned face and met the boy's bright, accusing blue eyes which glared so fearlessly back at him.

There was a long moment in which His Lordship's expression was too complicated for Rhodd to understand. But then he brushed Gar's fingers from his sleeve like dirt. 'Keep your hands off me, you filthy brat!'

Bethan shoved her way forward and grabbed Gar.

'Filthy brat, is he?' She spat the words into Lord Stanley's face. 'Your own son?'

An excited gasp went round the villagers. There had

long been gossip about who Gar's father might be, ever since Bethan came back from working at the Manor, but His Lordship? Now that really was a juicy gobbet of scandal for them to chew on!

Bethan did not stop. 'Your son . . .' she said again. Nothing to lose now. 'His name is Gar, though you never so much as bothered to find out,' she hissed. 'The schoolmaster says he's a smart boy. Cleverest lad he's ever taught. But he'll have no hope in life if you do this – taking away his home, closing the school! Book learning is his only chance to make something of himself!'

'*Your* son is no concern of mine.' Lord Stanley's shiny face was a nasty shade of puce as he hastily pulled himself up into the carriage, pulling a lace handkerchief from his pocket to wipe away the spittle.

'Drive, man!' he bellowed at the groom, and the footman leaped hurriedly on to the back of the carriage. Rhodd flinched with the horses' pain as the whip flicked down on to their wide backs and they jerked into a canter.

Cerys put her arm around Gar's mother. Bethan had slumped against her son after her outburst, dazed, barely able to stand. She had kept her secret safe for so long. But there would be no sympathy nor mercy in the village for her now.

Around them, the mood of the crowd was turning dark. They were looking for someone to blame.

'Hussy!' someone muttered.

'Always knew she was no better than she should be, that one,' added another woman.

'Leave her be!' Ma spoke up, though her voice was as soft as ever. 'It is His Lordship who should feel shame, not Bethan. Leaving his son fatherless and the boy's mother without a penny to her name.' She grabbed Gar and Rhodd with her free arm. 'Come on, children.'

Anger was engulfing the crowd like wildfire. With His Lordship gone, it hadn't taken long for them to find their scapegoats. Now they turned on Cerys too.

'Nothing's been right in this place since you took that creature in!'

The mutters gathered, flickering out of control.

'She's a stranger too – she weren't never from these parts neither!'

'What do we even know 'bout where she come from? Foreigner, she is.' Foreigner was the word they used for anyone not born and bred in the village. It was what they called outsiders.

Women's words were whipping up the flames and now the men stepped forward. They glowered down on Cerys, who squared her thin body to them as Bethan and the children clung to her.

'Cowards!' she yelled in their faces. 'You never said a word against me whilst my husband was alive – you'd never have dared.'

A couple of the men who had known her husband and travelled the seas with him stepped back, shamed, but then at last one of the women whispered the word – the word Cerys had always dreaded.

'Witch . . .'

The word was out. It hissed and cooled in the air and more hisses spread from it like snakes.

'That creature, that ain't no natural child . . .'

'It's a witch's familiar, it is, what does her evil bidding!'

'It's her familiar an' it's spreading the Sickness!'

'Witch! Witch! Witch!'

The first stone struck Rhodd's cheekbone. She touched the pain and was staring at the blood on her fingers when Ma grabbed her arm and tugged her away.

'Run, Rhodd, run!' she cried.

Bethan came to her senses at last and ran after them, pulling Gar behind her. A hail of stones followed them down the street.

'Faster, Gar,' Rhodd panted.

There was a snarl of anger gathering in the belly of this place. In Rhodd's mind it had become a savage beast. And it was only a matter of time until it tore her limb from limb.

She looked up, but the sky was empty. For the first time in her life, she was in danger and her falcon was nowhere to be seen.

CHAPTER 15

'What are you doing, Rhodd?'

Gar was glowering at her from the back door. She hadn't heard him knock nor come in through the front door. Ma must have let him in. She looked down, not wanting to see his accusing stare.

Rhodd was in the garden, playing with the otter pups. They had opened their eyes and were chasing each other with chuckling cries, in and out of a shallow water trough in the garden. They were Rhodd's only comfort in a world that had fallen silent around her.

No falcon. No Red. No birds. No creatures. Just silence.

She knew what Gar was asking and she didn't want to answer. The truth was she was doing nothing. But the nothing-doing was eating away at her like a dog gnawing at a bone.

Rhodd could smell the despair on Gar. School was the only hope Gar had ever had, the only hope of escape from the village. She had hardly seen him in the days that had passed since the meeting.

The mob had chased them home and showered their front doors with stones for hours, chanting and spitting out their hatred. Until at last they had got tired of their scapegoats and drifted off to worry about where they would go and what they would do once Lord Stanley evicted them from their homes. Now and then, a few of them returned to hurl abuse and rotting food as a way of venting their anger. Not a pane of glass was left unbroken in the windows of the cottages.

'Hopefully they've got other things on their minds than burning witches and shaming poor abandoned girls,' Cerys had muttered, her mouth a grim line as she swept up the glass.

But neither she nor Bethan had dared set foot outside since that day, and they kept their children close. Now more than ever, they were outcasts. They were living on whatever vegetables they had left and sharing the milk and cheese from Ma's goat and a few eggs from Bethan's chickens. And the days crept by towards the end of the month and the birds kept falling from the sky.

'I'm looking after the pups,' Rhodd replied to Gar's question at last. Her chin was set, defiant, but she kept her eyes fixed firmly on the baby otters. She couldn't look at him.

'But what are you *doing*?' Sharp as a sword double-edged with anger.

'Nothing.'

'That's right. Nothing. You're doing nothing. Just hiding away here.'

'I'm looking after the pups . . . The otter told me.'

'She told you more than that, though, didn't she?' Gar snarled. Rhodd had never told him what the otter had said but it wasn't just book learning that made Gar smart. 'There's something badly wrong – you can smell death all over the village,' Gar went on. 'Plants, birds, animals . . . people. And I don't really understand any of it, but I reckon you're the only one who can do anything to stop it.'

It was pouring out of him in an angry torrent now. 'Open your eyes, Rhodd! In four days' time none of us will have a home. Maybe you don't care. Maybe you've never cared about the rest of us. But even your ma's sick – and you're doing nothing!' He paused for breath, but he was still angry. And then he added quietly, the bit that hurt Rhodd most, 'Perhaps they're right, what they say . . . that you don't belong here.' Gar turned on his heel and left her.

The darkness that had slipped between Rhodd and Gar was yawning into a chasm.

The house seemed doubly gloomy when Rhodd stepped indoors and out of the scorching sunlight. She was brooding on what Gar had said. It was true that she cared very little about what happened to any of the other villagers, apart from Gar and Bethan. Why should she care if they all lost their homes? None of them had ever shown her any kindness. But she did care very much about Ma.

The familiar perfect oval of Ma's face blurred as if she was disappearing before Rhodd's very eyes. Rhodd panicked until she put her hands to her cheeks and felt wet stuff. It was only her tears. She brushed them away.

Ma was sitting shivering in her chair. She was doing nothing to pack or prepare to leave the cottage. Perhaps she didn't have the strength. Perhaps she reckoned that there was no need to find another place to live. Perhaps something had told her that this would be her last home.

Red had heaped himself over her feet to keep her warm, in the way he always did now. He whined, and Rhodd had to blink away more wet stuff as she saw Ma through the old dog's devoted gaze. Cerys's jet-black, luxuriant hair was turning grey, framing what had once been the loveliest face in the village. Now it was pinched with a low, devouring fever. But the green eyes turned on Rhodd were bright, with love enough to burn.

Ma! A voice wailed in Rhodd's head. It was the voice of the three-year-old who had walked out of the marsh into a pair of loving arms. *Not the Sickness, Ma . . .*

Rhodd had known the truth all along, of course, like a dog that smells disease in its owner long before anyone thinks about calling a doctor. It was what Red had been trying to tell her, but she hadn't let herself listen. Ma's strength was waning. It was like watching a mighty tide being drawn out by the moon.

'Death.' That's what Ma had said when she burned the hazelnuts and gazed into the fire. Was it her own death she had seen?

What are you doing, Rhodd?

Rhodd looked behind her, expecting – almost hoping – to see Gar's accusing face again. But Gar was gone. It was

Red asking that question now. His brown eyes were as accusing as Gar's blue ones had been.

You told me to keep myself safe... Rhodd heard herself whining in reply. **That's what you said when I used to sleep between your paws, outside, when I first came here**...

And then, all at once, she hated herself. Hated herself for whining, hated herself for clinging on to fear like that frightened child who walked out of the marsh all those years ago.

You are strong enough now, Rhodd, Red replied. **It is time.**

It was what her falcon had told her, but she hadn't listened. And now it might be too late.

There was wet stuff trickling down Rhodd's cheeks again and she turned away from Ma to hide it. She picked up the poker.

No more fear, she told herself. The flames leaped up at the poker's touch but she forced her body not to flinch. Took a step closer to the fire. Kept herself there until the heat hurt. Until she felt it burning, singeing the hairs on her arms. *Courage, girl!*

She wanted it to hurt. She had kept herself safe for too long.

'Ma . . .' Forcing her voice to stay steady. 'It's the Sickness, isn't it?' Neither of them had said it out loud until now.

Ma nodded. Sparing herself words as if they cost too much of her ebbing energy. Her tide was almost out.

'You have brought me such happiness, Rhodd.' Ma was struggling to find the strength to say the important stuff. 'You are a gift that has brightened every day of my darkness, since I lost Rhys to the marsh. Remember that, whatever is to come.'

It sounded like a farewell.

CHAPTER 16

Rhodd was trying to form words but she couldn't. Her head was filled with swirling shapes, the shapes of sadness. She could not even bear to look at Ma.

She wandered aimlessly about the cottage whilst the kettle boiled, brushing her fingers over the familiar pots and pans, the few bits of furniture they had left. Within days this home – the only home she had ever known – would be gone. But it was just a place. What really mattered was Ma. And the creatures that were depending on Rhodd. How to help? It all seemed impossible.

Her alphabet book was on the table where she'd left it, weeks before. Neither she nor Ma had even bothered to dust it. Rhodd picked it up. The lines and curves of the letters still winked at her defiantly, refusing to yield up their secrets. She shook her head and wrapped the book carefully in a piece of old cloth before putting it away in a drawer. All that was over, now.

'None of that stuff ever mattered to me, you know, Rhodd.'

Firelight glinted in Ma's eyes. She was watching her wild child. 'You have other gifts. It's up to you to use them.'

Rhodd could still say nothing. She carried over Ma's tea but she couldn't bear to look at her. She curled herself around her feet, next to Red, and dug her fingers deep into his fur.

At last she found words but they escaped as a wail. 'What can I do, Ma?' Who else was there to ask, with her falcon gone? This silent world was so lonely. 'What can I do – how can I make you well again, Ma?'

'Wash away the marsh, Rhodd,' came the answer.

Rhodd looked up at her for the first time. Was Ma joking?

Cerys *was* smiling – but only at Rhodd's bewilderment. Her voice was deadly serious. 'All the evil that has befallen this village – the Sickness, the death – it comes from the marsh,' she went on. 'Washing it away is the only way to get rid of it.'

She put her cup down and drew Rhodd's head towards her, kissing the top of her head. Rhodd's mass of hair tumbled loose and filled Ma's lap like a haystack of gold.

'Wash away the marsh, Rhodd,' Ma said again gently, stroking and taming Rhodd's mane. 'And bring back the river.'

Rhodd pulled her head free to stare at Ma. Her mother was still smiling even though her eyes were full of tears.

'How?' But it wasn't doubt that was making her ask. *Bring back the river.* Something was bubbling up in her chest like a mountain spring.

Ma didn't answer her directly. Her green eyes, huge in her gaunt face, glittered and sharpened as they looked into her daughter's black irises. 'Have I ever told you the story of Hafren, Rhodd?'

Rhodd shook her head. *Hafren.* It sent a shiver to her soul. No word had ever had meaning for her until this word.

'Hafren.' She repeated it again, in a whisper. Her eyes had widened into dark pools and Ma caught a rare glimpse of the yellow rims beneath her thick lashes.

'Men call Hafren's story a myth,' Ma said softly. 'But men call many things myths when they do not understand them. When they have forgotten their meaning.'

'Hafren . . .' Rhodd said it again and again – 'Hafren, Hafren' – as if she could not say it enough. She had the look of a wild creature when its whiskers brushed against some once-familiar place or caught the old scent of a long-loved mate.

Ma went on, 'Hafren was the daughter of King Locrin, who ruled over the Britons many long centuries ago. She was born in secret to his lover, a foreign princess named Estrildis. But King Locrin's wife found out. And in her anger, she ordered her manservant to murder Estrildis and the child. It was her way of getting her revenge on Locrin.

'The man killed Estrildis, but he could not bear to kill her innocent child with his own hands. Instead, he threw Hafren into the river. The river bore her body away and she was never seen again by mortal eye. But for ever after, that river was named Hafren. So that the princess should never be forgotten.'

'So she – Hafren . . .' Rhodd breathed the name with her whole body. 'She is . . .' She tailed off, not knowing how to say it.

'Hafren became the goddess of that river – *our* lost river, Rhodd. And they say that in times of trouble, she sends her spirit out from the waters, in the form of a . . .'

'A falcon.' Rhodd finished it for her. Ma nodded. There

was a thud of recognition in Rhodd's heart. It was like hearing something that she had always known out loud for the first time.

Cerys's eyes were closing. Rhodd shook her gently, and Red growled. But Rhodd ignored him. She needed to know more. She wailed, 'Ma! Tell me what to do!'

'You must have courage, Rhodd,' came the answer. It was what Ma had told her so many times. But this time it felt different. 'You must free the river.' Her voice was so faint, Rhodd had to bend close. 'You . . .'

But the last word faded on Ma's lips. She had slipped away, exhausted, into the dreams in which she searched for ever for her lost son.

Late that evening, Rhodd flung open the door to the cottage and looked out. The marsh stretched before her, swallowing darkness into itself, taking possession of the night. The moon was nothing but a whisper, shrouded by cloud.

She had lifted Ma's unconscious body on to the bed, light as air in her arms. Red was never allowed on the bed but tonight he had jumped up to lay his head on Ma's heart as if – by sheer force of love – he could keep it beating.

Rhodd had never felt so torn. Part of her was still that lost and frightened child, the child who had cleaved and clung to the mother who had taken her in – and that part of her told her she must stay at Ma's side, carry her to safety somehow, somewhere. Find another home for them both. But she knew that wasn't what Ma wanted.

Ma had been giving her permission to go, to leave her behind. She was pushing her out of the nest, forcing her fledgling to fly. Both of them knew that it might be too late to save Cerys from the Sickness. She had already lived longer than most of those struck down by it. But now she was telling Rhodd that a bigger task faced her and that she was the only one that could do it.

'*You* . . .' What had Ma been about to say?

Why did the name of Hafren send shivers through Rhodd? What did that name mean to her?

The dark sky had never seemed so big. It had never seemed so empty. No falcon soared above her head. The silence from the wild-ness pressed in on her. Nothing moved, nothing cried out. Whatever was out there was poisoning everything. This wasn't just about bringing back the river, it wasn't just about washing away the marsh. Deep down, Rhodd had always known that one day she would have to face the thing that held the marsh in its grip.

It would not give up its hold without a battle.

'Forgive me!' Rhodd called out to the earth. 'I am ready.' And then, like a prayer to the skies. 'Come back to me, my falcon. I cannot do this alone.'

But there was no answering cry. Just silence.

PART TWO

PART TWO

CHAPTER 17

Rhodd woke before dawn the next morning. She and Red were curled up together next to Ma. She held her breath for what seemed an age until she caught the sound of Ma's own shallow breathing.

She sat up. In three days, Ma would lose her home. But there might be even less time to save Ma's life. To stop the Sickness.

It was time to stop hiding here in the dark. It was time to act. She had to wash away the marsh and bring back the river. Not just for Ma, for the otters and all the other dying creatures. And she had to do it alone.

Rhodd slipped from the bed without waking Ma.

Stay with her, she told Red. It was agreed between them without the need for words.

When she stepped out of the back door, the goat heard her and bleated to be milked. Rhodd picked up the pail and went to kneel beside it, pressing her forehead against the creature's warm flank. The goat turned its head and butted Rhodd gently, as the milk frothed into the bucket from its full udders. It watched her with wise, bottomless brown eyes.

Drink. You will need strength.

Rhodd lifted the pail to her lips and drank down half the milk. *At least the goat is talking to me*, she thought. The warmth of the milk in her belly felt like a gift. Like approval.

The sun had not risen but the otter pups whimpered when they heard her moving about. She poured out the rest of the milk for them and they tumbled over each other in their eagerness to reach it. They were still learning to drink from the bowl and at first they dunked their heads down too deep and came out snorting and spluttering, grey muzzles dripping and coated with cream. But they learned quickly. Like all young things, the desire to live beat strong in their hearts.

Gar will look after you, she told them, but they were still too little to understand, too little for her to be able to explain another abandonment. **Look after them,** their mother had told her. Rhodd felt a twinge of guilt about leaving them. But if she didn't act, there would never be a home for those babies to go back to. And she knew they would be safe with Gar.

Rhodd went back into the cottage. Red's eyes shone in the darkness as he watched her moving about, cleaning and tidying. She worked quietly, not wanting to disturb Ma. The chores seemed more pointless than ever – soon every house in the village would be demolished if Lord Stanley had his way. But she wanted to leave everything just as Ma would want to wake up to.

She looked up at the spiders and they whispered to her in their dry rasping voices. After the silence from the creatures of the marsh, it was a relief to hear them. Soon they'd be able to weave cobwebs to their heart's delight.

You can cover the whole village with webs and nobody will care, Rhodd told them.

Rhodd packed up half the remaining store of little goat's cheeses, some apples and fistfuls of spinach, the dry heel from a loaf of bread. Slipped in Ma's sharp knife. Just in case. But at last, there was nothing more to be done.

Red lifted his head. **It is time.** It sounded like a rebuke. He knew she was just inventing jobs now.

Blinking hard, Rhodd went over and buried her face in Red's thick coat and then she lifted her head to look at Ma, who was still sleeping. Rhodd touched her face and whispered, soft as breathing, 'I will bring back the river, Ma. I will wash away the marsh and the Sickness.' She thought she saw a smile flicker there but Ma did not wake.

I will come back to you, she almost added. But something stopped her. She knew she could not make that promise. And she knew that Ma didn't expect it.

Rhodd forced herself to her feet. She went back outside and scooped the otter pups out of their water trough and into their basket. She tied a cloth over the top with string to stop them crawling out.

You are my messengers to Gar, she told them, though they were still too little to understand her mind-shapes. Gar would know to look after them.

Swinging her small bag of food on to her shoulder, she carried it and the basket out to the front and pulled the door gently closed behind her. There were no locks. 'Nowt worth stealing here.' That's what Ma had always said.

The basket of pups Rhodd left, mewling, outside Gar and Bethan's front door. They would soon wake and hear them. *And then Gar will know I am gone*, she thought. Bethan would look after Ma. They would take Ma with them when they left. If Rhodd did not return.

She paused for a moment, almost willing Gar to open

the door, just to see his face again. Loneliness gaped like a great hole inside her. They had always shared their adventures, until now.

Bitter thoughts whispered in her head. *Well, you wanted me to go, didn't you? You said maybe people were right, that I didn't belong here.* She turned away, trying to be angry with Gar. But she couldn't help remembering the rest of his words. *You're the only one who can do anything to stop it.*

It was true, what Gar said. She'd stuffed her ears for too long, kept her eyes closed to what was happening to the earth for too long. And Ma wasn't the only one who was paying the price with her life. Everything was dying.

Wash away the marsh, Ma had said. *Bring back the river*. The task facing Rhodd felt as huge as the grey, threatening skies above her head.

Out of habit, Rhodd looked up, hoping against hope that her falcon might be there, might have returned to help her. But there was no tug on her soul from above. The thread between them was snapped.

'How can I see what to do?' she whispered. Without her falcon's clear-sighted gaze, she was blind.

Go up! came an answering whisper. **Go up! Go up!**

It was not the voice of her falcon. She could not tell

whether it was the voice of the earth beneath her bare feet or the wind on her face or the salt water trickling down her cheeks. But she could hear love in the voice. And she knew it was a voice she must obey.

If your falcon will not come to you, you must climb up to him. See how he sees, even if it has to be without his eyes. You must see for yourself now.

There was a man-made road that curved up from the far end of the high street, leading to the world beyond. That was the road which had brought Lord Stanley's carriage into the village. But it was not a road Rhodd had ever thought to take, and nor did she think of taking it now. The answers she needed did not lie the way of men.

She looked up. Behind the cottages soared steep cliffs that Rhodd had never dared to scale. The village children sometimes scrambled on the lower rocks and jumped off, for a dare. Rhodd had never wanted to climb up, for fear of what she might see from the top. But now she needed to see.

She had to solve the secret of what had happened to the lost river before she returned to the marsh. Before she took on the dark force that had driven her from the wild.

In her mind, a shape was forming.

Hafren.

It was giving her new strength, strength she had never had before. But she did not need to spell it out as a word.

CHAPTER 18

Thunderclouds towered over the marsh as she headed towards the cliffs – black, threatening, drawing darkness up out of the wilderness. There was no visible horizon behind her. Mud met sky, seamless, in an eerie grey half-light. It was early morning but the sun – wherever it was hiding – was helpless, impotent. It had been swallowed by the impending storm.

When she reached the base of the cliffs, Rhodd rid herself of the long smock Ma had always insisted she wore over her light undershirt. She could not climb in that. She smiled as she tore the hated garment off over her head, remembering Ma's voice. *You have to look respectable, Rhodd. Don't give them any excuse to gossip.* But villagers' gossip was the least of her worries now.

'Sorry, Ma!' It felt so good to be freed from those folds of coarse cloth, which had always seemed to wrap themselves round her legs just at the moment she needed to run.

'Always wondered whose side you were on,' she muttered to the smock as she trampled it beneath her feet. But then she gasped when she saw the livid marks swirling around her bare legs. They had been aching for days but she had never before seen them so purple and angry, so stark against her pale flesh.

'Battle scars.' A half-memory formed in Rhodd's mind. Slipping and slithering out of her mind's grasp. It was a glimpse of a life-and-death struggle that no small child could ever have won on its own.

'But this time I will win!' For the first time in her life a great surge of pride rose in her chest, pride in those dark marks. 'I'll never hide my scars again.'

With new determination, Rhodd fastened her bag of food on her shoulders and grasped the first handhold and set her toes on the first foothold. It was her ladder to the sky. She pulled herself up.

The rain started as soon as Rhodd set foot on the cliff-face. But to call it rain did not come close to describing the deluge. After months of drought, it was as if all the water in the world had waited for this moment to fall to the earth, with the sole aim of washing Rhodd away to her death.

A crash of thunder shuddered overhead. It sounded as if something had broken in the heavens. The sandstone became gritty beneath her fingerholds; grains of sand worked themselves under her nails and between her bare toes and clung to her lashes and stung her eyes. Her undershirt clung to her wiry body until – to any onlooker – she would have looked as naked as the day she walked out of the wild. But nobody was there to witness Rhodd's battle with the elements. The villagers were cowering indoors, fearing what fresh horrors might be unleashed upon them with every thunderclap.

'You will . . . not . . . stop . . . me . . .' Rhodd's breath came in gasps as she climbed. She was swimming against the current. It seemed that some primeval beast was harnessing the storm, whipping up the wind, intent on preventing her from reaching the top. The rumbles of fury grew louder when she refused to give up. Jags of lightning struck at the cliff-face, threatening to split the ancient rock along its fault-lines.

Rhodd climbed on, dogged, determined. The burning of her scars intensified but she just used the pain to spur herself on. Not even this rain could flatten her wild mane. Her bright hair drew the electrical charge to itself like a lightning conductor; it channelled and tamed its force and became a torch that challenged the brilliance of each strike, throwing off white-gold sparks against the dark cliff.

You were born for this battle. Rhodd could not tell whose voice she was hearing; it was not the voice of her falcon, but it spoke straight to her heart. **You have a task to do.**

There were no creatures in this place that could be offering her their comfort. This voice was urging her on – **Fight! Fight!** – and pouring pure courage into her soul.

On and on she climbed. There were sections where the sandstone strata were kind to her and she could get her breath, places with layers as even and easy as the treads of a staircase. But then there were gaps where the only thing to do was to leap and hope and trust that she would land safe and that the wet sandstone would not crumble beneath her toes, sending her tumbling to her death.

And then came the moment when hoping and trusting were not enough. Rhodd slipped. The fingers of her right hand missed the hold – the sandy surface was too loose and soft to grip. Her left hand, taken by surprise, could not support her.

And she fell.

Her arms flailed, impotent, as if they were reaching out in longing to become wings. But she was no bird. Her knees and elbows were scraped raw as she hurtled down the hard-won rocks she had just climbed. Her fall was gathering speed. She opened her mouth to scream . . . only for the breath to be knocked out of her before any scream could escape.

Quite suddenly, gravity had lost its hold on her. Something had caught her, something held her for precious moments, long enough to grab handholds, secure footholds. And to breathe.

It was the sharp thrusts of thorns in her flesh that told her she had landed in a hawthorn bush. It was the only scrap of life that had been able to cling on to that wind-blasted cliff. And it had saved her.

'Thank you,' Rhodd whispered out loud to the hawthorn. But her last shreds of courage and strength had carried on falling without her and had landed somewhere at the bottom of the cliff. She made the mistake of peering down to look for them and her belly lurched with dizziness.

Rhodd wrenched her eyes away, forced herself to look upwards instead. A great yawning gap lay between her and the overhanging slab of stone above her head. If she jumped and missed . . . There was no doubt in her mind that her next slip would be her last. And then nobody could stop the Sickness, nobody would wash away the marsh and bring back the river.

Oh, for your wings!

Rhodd longed then for her falcon, for his effortless grip on the edge of the wind that would have taken her soaring to the top in the space of a single breath. But he was gone. She had lost that easy way through her blind cowardice. This was the price she must pay.

She was frozen now. Paralysed by fear. There was no going down nor up.

I can't do this! Help me!

She was calling out to any creature that might be her guide, whose eyes she could borrow, whose skin she could slip into.

How do I do this?

She sent the words out to the wild world, begging for help. But the hostile rock face was empty of life – apart from the hawthorn – and she had never spoken to trees. She wasn't even sure she could. There had been hardly any trees in the village – all chopped down for firewood – and before that, she had no memory of trees on the wind-blasted marsh. Could trees talk?

She felt a savage jab from the hawthorn's long spikes. Was that an answer?

Rhodd listened, caught the whisper of its leathery leaves. **Stop thinking.**

She wasn't alone.

But if I fall . . . If I fall, I will die.

The hawthorn leaves whispered again. **No animal thinks of death. Animals trust to their limbs, trust to their senses. And act.**

Rhodd gave herself a shake, like a dog emerging from a river. A spray of droplets cascaded from her body. It wasn't just the rain she was shaking off. She was shedding human layers, shaking off the years since she emerged from the wild.

Stop thinking, the hawthorn had told her.

She had been too long unwilded. She had to become that quivering ball of instincts once more.

'Just be,' she told herself, speaking the words out loud to make herself listen. She shook her head again to rid herself of human words. She must no longer use words. Words would not help her here.

The shape of a squirrel leaping across that gap gathered in her mind.

Be squirrel.

And she leaped.

Rhodd landed, clung to the jutting rock and bared her teeth in a feral grin. She was bubbling with sheer joy – joy in the ability of her own body to survive, to do her bidding. She pulled herself up. And then, without pause or thought she leaped again, on and up, a wild creature once more. It was instinct alone that told her where to aim the next foot, where to place the next hand.

Until with one last heave she hauled herself over the clifftop.

CHAPTER 19

Deep puddles had gathered at the top of the cliff and Rhodd threw off her bag and lay down and rolled in the thick mud until it coated every bit of her bare skin.

It was a return. A rewilding.

She tore at her thin undershirt, needing to feel more of the mud against her body. She had a desperate hunger to be heart-deep in the earth once more. If she could have done it, she would have ripped away her own smooth flesh – in the hope that she might find sleek fur or feathers beneath, in the desire to be nothing but animal.

She shrieked to the wild wind and to the rain and the thunder clouds over her head and howled to the dark earth that wrapped itself around her exhausted limbs and held her close. It was the language she had forgotten. Until, at last, the frenzy left her. Panting, spent, she lay still.

This time, Ma wasn't here to soothe Rhodd, to bring her back to the human, to remind her that she was not just animal, she was child. But after all those years away from the wild, human words were still lodged in Rhodd's head and they would not let her forget her mission. She must find the river.

Get up and look, the words told her.

She sat up slowly. She wiped the sticky mud from her eyes and peered at her reflection in a puddle. Thick black lines streaked down her pale cheeks. And her sun-bright hair, stiffened by sweat and earth, stood about her head like a dark crown of feathers.

What do I look like? And then it came to her.

It was the face of a falcon. She was Peregrine. The face that stared back at her was savage, merciless. She did not know this Rhodd. But she liked her better than the tame, timid Rhodd who had hidden away so long from her fears.

Here on top of the cliff, she was almost as high as a hawk. *Surely I will see what he sees now?* she thought. Rhodd made herself get to her feet. And, finally, she made herself look down at the marsh, spread out below.

She breathed out. She'd been holding her breath but now she let the breath go. Because she saw . . . nothing.

Beneath her all was grey, lifeless. A grey shroud of rain hid the truth that she needed to see. Grey reeds, grey mud, grey water, reflecting grey skies above. She still only had her human eyes. She could not see far enough to find the thing that some deep-buried memory told her was lurking there. And she still could not see the river.

The shape of the shifting ditches swirled and slithered through the marsh in barely perceptible patterns. Grey on grey. Those patterns reminded her of something on the edge of thought, something she could not yet grasp. Something long locked away from memory. But of the river she saw nothing. No shining arrow to the sea. She didn't know what she had expected to see, but there were no answers here.

I need your eyes!

Rhodd was sobbing into the wind. She was calling for her lost falcon. Without him there was a great hole in her heart. But the wind did not bear back that beloved shape, carving through the air. She was still alone and did not know where to look.

She turned her back on the marsh, her heart sick and sinking. Ahead of her – to the east, where the sun rose – stood a range of hills and valleys even higher than the cliff she stood on, distant, lost in a blued blur. The river might be hidden in any of those valleys. And there was so little time left, so little time to stop the Sickness and save Ma.

Go up! Go up! That voice again.

Rhodd sighed. She would have to go higher. What else could she do?

CHAPTER 20

At first it was all Rhodd could do just to put one foot in front of the other, to persuade herself that she was making progress towards the blue hills. She was exhausted, her legs still shaking from the climb. And she didn't want to think how many of those hills she would have to face before she found the river.

The rain at least had stopped. But after a while an eerie silence crept into her ears and made her listen. In spite of the rain, the earth beneath her feet felt hard as iron, as if it had been robbed of water for a long time. Between her bare toes, straggly grass and wild flowers were rotting, stinking and slimy. No bright butterflies patterned the sky with colour. This place was as barren as the village below the cliff.

Here there should be sweet meadows where skylarks soared and swooped on the liquid scales of their own songs. But all was silence. No fat contented rumbling of wood pigeons. No rustling of mice and voles along secret tunnels in long grass. Everything was dead or dying here too.

Until then, Rhodd had been walking up an incline, but now the ground sloped away in front of her, revealing a great house on the other side of a shallow valley. The mansion was built from smooth cream stone rather than the rough red sandstone quarried in these parts, and it was grander than anything she had ever seen in her life. It was so tall Rhodd wondered for a moment whether whoever lived there could see the truth about the river from its top windows.

'If you piled up all the houses in the village on top of one another it still wouldn't make a house as high as that,' Rhodd muttered to herself. 'And you'd need even more to fill out the sides.' She was talking out loud because she was sick of the silence. 'Gar would know how many.' It was the sort of calculation Gar would enjoy, she thought with a pang of loneliness.

The house was a puzzle to her. Who lived there? As if in answer, a jaunty yellow carriage bowled up the long gravel drive and swept to a halt outside the double flight of steps at the front of the house. A man dressed elegantly in black stepped down from the carriage and stalked up the steps. Lots of servants, all alike in dark green uniforms, buzzed like drone bees around the horses and up the steps behind him.

Lord Stanley's house, then. *But he's just one man. Why would he need a house that big?* There were more windows than she could count, just on the side she could see. It didn't make sense. *He would have plenty of room for Gar,* she thought. *Why can't Gar go and live there, if he is his son?* And then she thought a bit more. *In fact, why not the whole village? They could all live there and room to spare.*

That idea made her giggle, because even without Ma explaining it to her, Rhodd knew that wasn't ever going to happen. People had lots of rules about stuff like that. Rules Rhodd would never understand.

But it all made her even more sure that Lord Stanley was a liar. *He said he needed money,* she thought. *But that can't be true, living in a house like that.* Then she remembered that slither of something shameful, like an eel, under the sleek smoothness of his face. It was when he'd told the villagers that nobody knew what had happened to the river.

'He was lying,' Rhodd told herself with new certainty. 'Lord Stanley knows the truth.'

Rhodd walked on, cautious now. Everything told her that Lord Stanley was not a man to be trusted.

The mansion sat above gentle sloping grounds, as if it was balanced on the rim of a saucer – below it lay a dried-up lake. The effect of the expensive landscaping was spoiled by the brown, scorched look of the lawns. The grass was all dead or dying. Carefully positioned trees had been scattered about the slopes and thickly planted on the upper rim of the saucer. It felt artificial, nature tamed and tidily arranged so as to make a pleasing view from every window.

Rhodd had never seen nature bent to human whim like that. Nothing felt right about it. Her way ahead, towards the high hills, lay around the top edge of the saucer and through the woods. She made a dash for the trees – they would at least shield her from those staring windows. All of Rhodd's instincts were twitching, telling her to keep clear of the house. Everything here whispered 'danger'.

Before she plunged into the cover of the little wood, a faint warmth on Rhodd's back told her that the sun was setting in the west. She turned to look, but the sunset was hidden in heavy clouds. 'The sun's still there,' she whispered. Remembered Ma's promise to a small frightened child. *The sun always rises, Rhodd.*

Ma used to tell her how – before the marsh spread – she

and her son, Rhys, always watched the sun slipping into the sea in the evening. 'The sun on the sea . . . it was the most beautiful thing you could imagine, Rhodd. A blazing ball of flame setting fire to the water. But then every night, it was swallowed into the waves.' She'd sighed.

'That's why people are scared of the night,' Ma went on. 'Because there is always the fear that the water might have drowned the sun, and the light and the warmth will never return. But then we watch through the long hours of darkness and we wait and we hope and we set our eyes to the east. And the sun always rises.'

The dusk was gathering around Rhodd. *Animals aren't scared of the night,* she comforted herself as she was swallowed into the thickening darkness under the trees. *They know in their bones that the sun will return.*

But then a scream of pure terror rent the shadows. Rhodd stopped dead. It was an animal in pain, in terrible pain.

CHAPTER 21

Where are you?

Rhodd was trying to break through the creature's fear, to see through its eyes so that she could find it, but its terror was too great. It was blocking out her mind-shapes. She could do nothing but follow its cries.

Dry leaves crisped thick beneath her feet as she ran, casting about with her ears to find the shrieking creature. The trees above were shedding their green life already, even though it was still summer. The smell of decay, sweet but sickening, rose with every step. Even the trees were dying.

She tried again. **Where are you?**

This time, like a sob, a voice came back to her. **Here. The thing that bites but does not eat has me in its**

jaws ... Help me ...

Rhodd turned on her heel to follow the voice. She was about to plunge on instinct into the scrubby undergrowth but as she swivelled round a sharp stone stabbed into her foot. It made her pause for a moment. A reminder that she must think first.

What bites but does not eat? she asked herself. She shivered. Animals bite only to defend themselves, only kill when they are hungry, only eat to survive. So – something made by man, then. She had been right when she sensed that this place was dangerous. She must be careful.

Do you have night eyes? Rhodd asked.

The shrieks had turned to whimpers. **Yes.**

Show me. Show me what you see.

Her focus switched and she saw again through another creature's eyes. She almost sobbed herself with the sheer joy of it. But there was no time for that.

Over the creature's head towered tall stalks – what were they? She sniffed with its nose. It was the smell of bracken, dead or dying – brittle brown leaves where there should have been the soft green fronds of summer.

I am coming. Don't give up. Rhodd could feel the creature's strength ebbing. Cautiously, on alert for the thing that bites but does not eat, she crept forward into the undergrowth.

She could not stop herself from sobbing when she found the poor creature. The pity was overwhelming.

A young rabbit lay panting on its side, one of its hind paws trapped in the jaws of a monster. It was a monster made of metal, with teeth sharp as a hawk's talons. Savage, cruel. But this thing did not kill clean like her falcon. It did not kill to live. It was a dead thing, made by man.

Rhodd wiped her wet face, impatient with herself. The rabbit was struggling and with every desperate struggle the teeth bit deeper.

Try to lie still, Rhodd told it.

But it hurts so . . .

Let me think.

Rhodd had to untangle her own thoughts from the rabbit's thoughts, which were scrambled by pain and fear. Had to think like the human that had made this horror. She turned the shapes in her head back into human thoughts and wrapped her tongue around the words she had learned to use.

'You have to open it,' she muttered to herself. But then she checked her hands, pulled them back as they reached instinctively for the trap. 'Not like that, numbskull,' she scolded, frustrated by her own clumsiness. 'You'll trap your own fingers, and you'll be no use for anything. You need some sort of tool . . .'

She looked about, picked up a piece of wood, poked it between the teeth, rejected it. It was useless. 'Too soft.' She needed something hard, harder than metal.

'Oh!' she cried out in frustration. 'What would Gar do?' And all this time the rabbit's confusion and terror kept breaking into her mind. Every instinct was telling the animal to run away from the pain, but the pain was its own foot, part of its very being.

'Quickly, quickly!' Rhodd urged herself. She forced her mind to beat down the rabbit's panic, to think. 'Harder than metal . . . stone, then!' She remembered the sharp stab in her foot, back on the path.

I will be back, she promised.

Still cautious in case there were more traps hidden in the undergrowth, Rhodd used the rabbit's eyes to retrace her own steps through the dying bracken. A sharp flint lay amongst the leaves, glinting in the low light. She grubbed it up with her fingers and hurried back to the trapped creature. Its eyes were closed now and she placed her hand on its warm flank. Its breathing was shallow, sparse. It was giving up.

I'm here now. Trust me. You will live. It was not just a promise, it was a command.

Rhodd considered the trap with all her human-learned understanding. 'If I push it in there, I can prise it apart enough to . . .' Slowly, slowly, she worked the sharpest edge of the flint between the jaws of the trap. The teeth cracked apart, more, more. Until at last she jammed the stone in far enough to spring the trap open with a snap.

She lifted the mangled paw from the trap. It dangled limp and useless. Broken.

The rabbit took one look at it and fell back, despairing. **My paw . . . My poor paw.**

Rhodd opened her food bag and took out Ma's knife. **I have to do this. Trust me.**

With one swift slash through fur and bone and ligament she severed the broken foot. She quickly tore off a bit of her ragged undershirt and wrapped it around the wound to stop the bleeding.

Then she picked up the quivering rabbit and cradled it just as Ma had once cradled her.

You will run again, she told it. Beneath the soft fur her caressing fingers could feel no fat. The creature was no more than a bag of bones. **You're starving!**

There is nothing left to eat. My mother told me this

was once a good place to live. But the good grass is gone, less each year. And she is gone. Nothing left now.

Rhodd laid the wretched animal in her lap and opened the food bag.

Eat. She watched as the rabbit nibbled at some spinach and a bit of apple before falling asleep, exhausted.

Nothing left. That's what it had said. The curse of the lost river had not only fallen on the village, then.

'Tomorrow I will find the river,' Rhodd promised before she too fell asleep. Promised the rabbit in her lap and Ma lying sick in the dark cottage, promised her falcon and this dying world.

'And if not tomorrow, then the next day. I won't give up. I will keep going until I find it.'

CHAPTER 22

Rhodd slept light like a hawk, waking at the stirring of a leaf and the turning of a worm in the soil. It felt good to lie close to the earth once more, to breathe in its musky sweetness. The freedom of the wild seeped into her shallow dreams, which were different here, earthbound no longer, away from the village and under the wide skies.

But towards dawn a deeper sleep overcame her, so it was the rabbit that heard the dogs before she did. Its long ears twitched and it jerked up in her lap, ready to leap away. Until it remembered its missing hind paw and snuffled in misery.

It was the rabbit's snuffling that woke Rhodd. She soothed the rabbit and undid the bandage to check on the wound. It was a clean cut, and the bleeding had stopped.

She knew Ma would have poulticed it with herbs – but there was no greenery left alive here. She just had to hope it would heal.

The barking of the dogs reached her ears now. By the cast of the thin dawn light creeping through the treetops, Rhodd could tell it was very early. *Another night gone.* Only two days left until the evictions. She wondered how Ma was. *Bethan's looking after her,* she told herself. But fear added quietly, *If she is still alive . . .* Surely she would know if Ma was gone, surely she would sense if that great spirit had left this world?

She shook her head free of such thoughts and listened. The sounds were distant. *Over by the house,* she thought. The dogs were barking a joyful morning chorus, in sheer delight that a new day had dawned and they were being freed from their kennels. But then came the harsh shout of a man and the barks turned to yelps of pain.

'Whipping them!' Rhodd growled and the hairs on the back of her neck bristled. 'Whipping them just for being happy.' This was a cruel place.

We should go, she told the rabbit. She picked up her bag and slung it over her shoulder. The rabbit hunkered into her chest, still quivering between her hands, and they set off through the woods. She was in no hurry. Why would the barking of Lord Stanley's dogs be any business of hers?

But ten minutes later, the barking was coming closer. **Can't you go faster with those ridiculously long legs?** snapped the rabbit.

Rhodd almost laughed, before she remembered the trap. *He'll be going to check it*, she realised, too late. She'd been too slow to make the connection. *Gar would have guessed*, she thought, cursing her own stupidity, and she broke into a run.

Too soon she heard the man's boots on dry leaves, crashing through the dead bracken, heard him cursing over the sprung trap. It wasn't the smooth aristocratic drawl of Lord Stanley. The gamekeeper, then. A man whose job it was to kill animals. *The one who pays the boys for killing birds, back in the village*, Rhodd thought.

A hunger rose in Rhodd's heart. A hunger for revenge.

'Summat's been at this trap,' she heard the gamekeeper telling the dogs. 'An' it ain't no fox. Foxes don't carry no knives.' He must have found the rabbit's cleanly severed foot. 'Blasted poachers,' he cursed again. 'Have at 'em, boys!' he yelled.

The dogs let out a full-throated baying and crashed through the bracken after Rhodd. They were following her scent. Hunting her.

They are coming after us. But Rhodd didn't need the rabbit to tell her that. The terrified animal was already struggling to leap out of Rhodd's hands, even though it stood no chance of escape on three legs.

Sorry about this, Rhodd apologised as she grabbed the creature firmly by the scruff of its neck and stuffed it into her bag. It would be safer there. As long as she could run fast enough to escape herself.

It was hard to run fast in the dim dawn light beneath the trees. The dead leaves were piled thick, concealing gnarled tree roots that made her stumble, losing valuable seconds. She scrambled to her feet. She could hear the dogs' frenzied, eager yelps as they scented their quarry close. They would be on her in moments.

Rhodd had run from the bullies plenty of times, back in the village. She knew what it was to be a creature hunted. But here in the wild she instinctively moved differently. Darting, swift, at one with the forest, using the soft dawn shadows to conceal herself. She was panting hard as she arrived in a clearing and cast about for some hiding place. The dogs worked by scent and they were faster than her.

They will catch me. She threw her fear out to the wild world. It was a desperate cry for help.

Up here, came a whisper overhead. It was the dry susurration of trees dying of thirst, almost leafless, weakened by drought. But still strong enough to help Rhodd. She stretched up her arms as she had once lifted them to her mother and a great grey-barked beech reached down its low boughs and lifted her, with the rabbit, out of the reach of the dogs. She swung herself higher, just as they burst into the clearing, just in time to escape the snatch of their snarling jaws.

The gamekeeper was still crashing behind them through the undergrowth, no more than a few minutes behind his dogs. Beneath the tree the pack gathered and howled in frustration.

Whose side are you on? Rhodd glared down at the slavering hounds, trying to break through their man-made bloodlust to speak to them. **Why would you help him? He is a cruel man, a bad man. He beats you, he kills creatures that have done him no harm . . .**

The dogs' howls turned to whines. **But he feeds us!**

Shame on you! Rhodd scolded and they whimpered, confused. **Now be off with you, she told them. Keep running and he will never know I was here.**

The dogs still hesitated. Their loyalties were torn by a lifetime's training. The man had almost caught up with them. If he caught Rhodd here, she would be locked up for poaching, for stealing His Lordship's property. *As if an animal could be property*, Rhodd raged to herself. But she knew all hope for Ma – for the river – would be at an end if she was captured.

Go! I have the lost river to find. A new voice swelled up from Rhodd's heart, commanding the dogs to obey a greater power. **In the name of Hafren.**

At that name a stillness fell and the wild wood held its breath. The dogs whimpered and bowed their heads in instant submission. Then they sprang away, moments before the gamekeeper ran into the clearing.

The man – red-faced, sweating – stopped. He stood for what seemed like an age underneath Rhodd's branch. She could see the dappled light glinting on the cold metal of a gun. This man could maim her, kill her, just as he had killed countless hundreds of the creatures that she loved. To her nose he had a human stink, a stink she now realised that she had stopped noticing after her first weeks in the village. *I had forgotten how I hated that smell.*

The gamekeeper bent and examined the disturbed leaves where the dogs had circled. *If he looks up, I am lost*, she thought. He clearly guessed that something had happened here. His dull human senses were puzzled.

Then the dogs let up a howl in the distance, and their master – her hunter – went after them.

CHAPTER 23

After the gamekeeper left to follow his hounds, Rhodd settled herself more securely, cross-legged on the broad branch, and opened the bag to allow the rabbit to poke out its head.

He's gone, she told it. **We're safe now.**

Maybe. Judging by the droop of its ears, the rabbit didn't seem too hopeful and she couldn't blame it, what with its maimed leg. But its eyes looked brighter and less sunken than the night before. It was on the mend.

Breakfast! We just need a bit of breakfast! she told the rabbit. It was the sort of thing Ma said when things were looking gloomy. And no matter how little food they'd had, she'd always rustled something up, from an egg and a bit of cheese and scraps of the previous night's leftovers.

I'm so hungry, Rhodd was chatting to the rabbit as she rummaged around in the bag. She dug out a crust of bread. But she couldn't find any of the spinach.

The rabbit was looking shifty. Its black eyes wouldn't meet hers. It hopped out of the bag and limped away along the branch to drink from a hollow full of rainwater next to the tree trunk, keeping its back turned to Rhodd.

Rhodd giggled. The rabbit had clearly decided to live and, after all, she didn't begrudge it a bit of spinach. She pulled out one of the goat's cheeses and ate that. The apples had been nibbled too, but at least the rabbit had left the cheese alone.

After she had eaten, Rhodd shuffled closer to the rabbit and scooped up some water from the hollow into her own mouth.

What happened to your mother? And the other rabbits?

The rabbit kept its back turned to her. **Gone away.**

Rhodd stroked its long silky ears. **I'm sorry.** It was not possible to tell in its simple language whether that meant they had moved on or they were dead. For the rabbit it was the same thing.

She pulled her bag closer and repacked the rest of the food. She popped the rabbit back in.

I can move quicker that way, she told it. **But don't eat**

everything whilst you're in there. We've still got a long way to go. The rabbit sniffed but it didn't argue.

Hoisting the bag on to her back, she slid down from the beech.

Thank you. She pressed her forehead against the smooth silver-grey bark.

Go safe, came the parched whisper. **Bring back the river. That is your task. None of us can live much longer, without it.**

The next few miles through the woodland were a revelation to Rhodd. Her loneliness without Gar was forgotten. She had spent her life listening to animals and birds, even insects, though she had never before attended to the complex conversations between trees. It was the language of the under-earth, the oldest language of all. For her it was the awakening of another sense, a sense she might once have known but had long forgotten, as she opened her mind to these unfamiliar tongues that never took on the shapes of words.

All around her were the whispers and mutters of ancient wisdom, humming through the sap that rose up through the trees' branches, exchanged through the intertwining of their thick roots, through the maze of fungal threads that carried messages beneath the earth.

Beneath her bare feet she felt the deep thrumming of life, woven into a great tapestry, connected. It was the warp and weft of the green earth and she was part of it. But it was fading.

We need the river. We need the river. There was a gasp of desperation at the edge of those voices. Her pace quickened. The rhythmic hum beneath the earth became her heartbeat and she could no more have abandoned her quest than she could have stopped herself from breathing.

The baying of the hounds and the shouts of their master had faded away and Rhodd felt safe, lulled by the soft light and cradled by the trees. But it could not last. She had reached the edge of the wood. She hesitated before stepping out of her cover and into the blast of the afternoon sun. Ahead of her lay another scorched hillside. Yesterday's rain had come too late for the dead grass.

Rhodd peered out. Her way lay up the hill ahead; it felt very exposed after the shelter of the trees. The windows of the mansion stared in every direction. *Anyone will be able to see me from there*, she thought.

There were no fences or walls in view, no boundaries to the estate that she could make a run for. 'Is all this Lord Stanley's land?' she wondered out loud even though there was nobody to answer. There was no point in asking the rabbit – it neither knew nor cared about that sort of thing. But she – with her human upbringing – understood that it mattered. Because as long as she was on Lord Stanley's land, the gamekeeper would keep coming after her, keep hunting her down.

'How much of the world can one man own?' Rhodd muttered furiously. It made no sense to her that any patch of earth could belong to a human being, but Gar had told her that it was so and therefore it must be true.

There was no other way. All her instincts told her to run and to keep running, but she could never maintain that pace all the way up that long hillside. So she stepped out of the wood and set off as fast as she could go, running for as long as her lungs could bear, then walking and stumbling the rest.

Rhodd's ears twitched. If she could have swivelled them like a cat or a dog, they would have been constantly shifting as she scurried over that open space. But she only had her own poor human senses to rely on. The rabbit was sleeping the deep sleep of healing. And it seemed to be the last creature left alive in this desolate place.

He's killed it all. Fury was building in Rhodd and she cursed Lord Stanley as she struggled up the hill. Whatever had happened to the river, she was sure now that he was somehow to blame.

She was halfway up the slope when she heard the hooves behind her. She looked back.

A horse was pounding towards her, carrying a heavy, thick-set man on its back. It wasn't a high-spirited thoroughbred horse like the fine pair of matched greys that had pulled Lord Stanley's carriage – this was a brown workaday hack, made for long hours covering miles of the estate. But it was fast, and the man on its back was the gamekeeper. After his bewitched hounds had led him a merry dance, he'd clearly given up on them and gone back to get his horse. He wasn't abandoning his hunt for the poacher who had robbed him of a rabbit. It was a matter of honour for him now.

Rhodd looked around. It was too late to run back and hide in the wood, too far to reach the top of the hill and find somewhere to hide.

The savage, desperate snarl of a creature at bay gathered in Rhodd's throat and she turned to face the man riding the horse. Her mane, still dark with mud, stood stiff about her head; her pale face was moustachioed with dirt and her black eyes flashed, stark-rimmed by yellow. She was pure Peregrine. And the wild skirling cry she made now – 'Airk, airk!' – was no sound that was ever made by human voice.

Startled at the sight of her, the gamekeeper pulled hard on the reins. He jerked the horse's head back so harshly that Rhodd heard a crack in its neck; the horse reared up, whinnying at the shock.

Do not fear me, Rhodd soothed the horse. **I am not your enemy. You are carrying your enemy upon your back. Rise up and rid yourself of him.**

To the gamekeeper she bared her teeth and she cried out again, '*Airk, airk!*' It was a cry from the depths of her wild heart.

'What are you?' The gamekeeper's eyes flickered with fear. In front of him he saw a semi-naked creature, its bare legs scarred with dark marks that looked like swirling stings and bites. Any remains of clothing were torn to shreds and plastered with mud. Surely no human child, this?

The man made the sign that Rhodd had seen Ma Johnson make weeks before – the sign to ward off evil. He spat out a foul curse. 'You are that creature from the village – the thing that crawled out of the marsh.'

Without a pause, he lifted his gun. He was aiming it straight at Rhodd's heart.

Rhodd stared back at him, still as a tree, drawing up courage from the under-earth. A cold defiant flame flickered in her black eyes.

Rise up, she told the horse calmly. **In the name of Hafren.**

At that name, the placid workaday hack – which had never once rebelled in all the years since it had been broken to reins and saddle as a colt – rediscovered the wild spirit of its ancestors that had once roamed free over these meadows. It reared high its front legs and then plunged down and bucked back its hind legs. The gamekeeper – unprepared for this act of mutiny – tumbled from the saddle just as he pulled the trigger. His shot went off harmlessly and was buried deep in the earth.

Rhodd didn't wait to see whether he got up. She just ran.

CHAPTER 24

From the groans that followed Rhodd up to the top of the hill, she reckoned the gamekeeper was still alive – and stirring. But hopefully he wasn't in any fit state to get up any time soon and follow her. She didn't wish him dead, but she rather hoped he might have broken something in his fall.

She could hear the hooves of his horse cantering away into the distance. It would not hang around to help him. It had heard the name of Hafren and it was her creature now.

But Rhodd also knew that once the horse was found, riderless, others would come in search of the gamekeeper. *He'll tell them that I'm here and they'll come after me*, Rhodd thought despairingly. She was still a creature on the run, she was still being hunted, and she was reaching the limits of her strength. But she could not rest. She had to get off Lord Stanley's land. Had to find the river.

Rhodd's life-and-death game of hide and seek with the gamekeeper had gone on for hours, and the light was already fading into evening, dimming into dusk. *Another day gone*, she thought despairingly. The rabbit was asleep again, so she must rely on her human eyes. She kept walking.

Rhodd had dragged her weary body across a field and up yet another hill before she saw the stone wall that marked the edge of the estate.

'At last!' She gritted her sharp little white teeth and they glinted, savage, in the half-light. 'They can't stop me, once I'm over that wall. It's not his land.'

But Lord Stanley's gamekeeper still had one last trick for unwanted intruders. As Rhodd summoned her final burst of energy to make a run for the wall, the ground gave way beneath her and she fell into the earth.

It was a man-trap, covered with bracken and designed to catch poachers coming over the wall. Rhodd hit her head hard on a rock at the bottom, landing heavily on her side. Only by twisting her body at the last moment had she narrowly avoided crushing the rabbit in the bag beneath her.

She tried to sit up, but the dizziness in her head and a stabbing pain in her ribs defeated her. *Broken*, she thought.

She laid herself back gingerly and looked up through the gap her body had made in the bracken. The pit must be six feet deep. It would have been an impossible climb – even with unbroken ribs. The sides of the pit were sheer, smooth earth. She realised with a shudder that there were animal bones scattered everywhere. *I won't be the first creature to die down in this pit.*

The old panic that she had felt years before at being shut inside, away from the open skies, away from her falcon, rose in her. 'No!'

She forced herself up on to one elbow and clawed at the pit sides with her free hand, over and over. Her shattered rib bones scraped against each other as she twisted and she was gagging with the pain. But the soft earth just crumbled under her fingers. There was no way to get a handhold and the agony of holding herself up soon became too much.

With a sob she fell back once more, dizzy and exhausted. All she could think now was that she would surely die here. There was no escape. The pain was making her woozy and it hardly seemed to matter now. Her human body had never felt so heavy, so earth-locked.

We're trapped, she told the rabbit as it poked its head

cautiously out of the bag. The fall had woken it. It rubbed its face vigorously with its front paws as if it was clearing its head after a nice long sleep. **I'm sorry.** But the rabbit didn't look too bothered about being at the bottom of a hole in the ground. And then she remembered it was, after all, a rabbit.

'Suppose you're used to it,' she muttered. In fact, the rabbit looked a lot better. Positively frisky. It had obviously slept well through all the adventures of the afternoon. *Good for you*, Rhodd thought to herself, a trifle bitterly. But she didn't say any of that to the rabbit. None of this was his fault.

Why don't you finish the apples? she suggested, kindly, instead.

Rhodd lay on her back and looked up with longing at the purpling of the evening sky. The moon was rising, a few shavings away from full, and the early stars were spinning in a perfect circle above her head.

As her consciousness slipped away, Rhodd was aware of nothing but the earth pressing in on all sides and the freedom of her falcon, somewhere, lost to her now. She ached to feel the old tug of the thread between them. If only she could rise into his feathers and his bones. If only she could be at one with him, wherever he was. Thinking as he thought, seeing as he saw.

Just one more time, she prayed. **Just one more time.**

Rhodd's last thoughts were of Hafren, before a great blackness took hold of her mind.

CHAPTER 25

'What the blazes are we doing, following a rabbit?'

Rhodd had no idea how much time had passed before she was woken by a voice high above her head. No idea how long she had been unconscious, except there was pink dawn light in the circle of sky, which she seemed to remember being full of stars. But she didn't believe she was really awake anyway, because it sounded like Gar's voice, and Gar was back in the village with the otter cubs and Ma and Bethan and Red and nowhere near this dark place she found herself in.

I'm dreaming, she thought. *Or else I must have hit my head really hard when I fell.* She remembered falling, although she didn't remember much else. She appeared to be at the bottom of a deep hole in the ground.

But the voice was still talking, and it really did sound like Gar. 'Blimey, I wish I could speak Rabbit like Rhodd ... then I'd know what the little blighter is making such a fuss about with all that snuffling and nose twitching ...'

Rabbit? What was it that rang a bell about a rabbit? *Wasn't there a rabbit down here in this hole with me when I fell asleep?* Rhodd looked around. No rabbit. She pulled her bag towards her, wincing at the pain in her ribs when she moved. She opened it. She could have sworn there had been a rabbit in there. But there was definitely no rabbit. Just a couple of goat's cheeses – untouched – what looked like the nibbled stalks of some apples, and a knife.

There was spinach in this bag, thought Rhodd, trying hard to concentrate. *And definitely a rabbit. A rabbit with a missing paw ... I rescued it ... There was a trap ... a man who was chasing me ... and dogs ... and a horse ...*

It was starting to come back to her in bits, like a jigsaw puzzle, but there were lots of pieces missing and the places where the gaps were felt fuzzy and blurred like she would never be able to join them up. And she felt very sick whenever she moved her head. The whole thing was far too much effort and Rhodd thought blearily how nice it would be to close her eyes and go back to sleep for a long time. She lay back again. Her ribs hurt less, lying down.

But that voice up there was talking again and it was keeping her awake. 'It'd be even better if I could talk Dog, wouldn't it, Red? But I reckon maybe that's the same thing anyway. Do all animals speak the same language, or is it like French and German and Russian and whatever? Should've asked Rhodd about that . . . Either way, Red, I've no idea why you insisted on us following this stupid rabbit when—'

'Gar?' Rhodd couldn't stop herself. Even if this was a dream – or a hallucination – she might as well join in. She shouted again, louder. 'Gar?' It even hurt to shout.

'Rhodd? Where are you?' A quick, eager response – it really did sound like him . . .

'Gar?'

At the sound of Rhodd's voice, frantic whines started up above her head and scrabbling paws sent clods of soil tumbling down the side of the pit.

Red? Is that you? Rhodd was still finding all this impossible to believe.

Yes, Rhodd, it's Red! We've found you! At last! I couldn't find your scent . . .

The digging got faster and more frenzied. **Hold on! I'll dig you out!**

171

Stop it, Red! It's not helping – it's too deep – and you're just covering me in soil!

The digging paused, replaced by eager snuffles of excitement and frustration.

How did you find me? It was easier for Rhodd to think when she wasn't being showered with earth.

A rabbit stopped us in the road, but the stupid creature didn't make much sense . . . It was blathering on about somebody being stuck down a hole and there being no spinach left . . . Red snorted. **Between you and me, I don't think it has got all its wits about it, but then I suppose it's only a rabbit. It seemed to want us to follow it. The boy took some persuading, though. Not sure he's that bright either.**

Rhodd couldn't stop herself snorting at Red's suggestion that Gar was stupid. He was the cleverest person she knew. She tried shouting to him again. 'Gar, is that . . . Gar? Down here! Watch out – it's . . . a trap! Don't fall in!'

'Rhodd!' Gar's face cautiously peered over the edge. 'Can you climb out?'

Rhodd shook her head and then remembered that Gar would need to see her to be able to understand a shake of the head, and it was very dark down here at the bottom. 'No . . . too high . . . and I'm hurt . . . !'

'Right, we'll need to get something to help pull you out . . .' She didn't need to see Gar's expression to know that his familiar puzzling-out frown would be creasing deep between his eyebrows.

'Hurry, Gar! The gamekeeper – trying to catch me . . . need to get off . . . Lord Stanley's land . . . before he comes back!' It wasn't just her broken ribs that were making her words so halting. Human words felt unfamiliar, strange in her mouth after her return to the wild.

'Don't worry – I won't be long – Stay with her, Red.'

The sound of Gar's footsteps, running off. Then silence.

Red? Rhodd could hardly bear to ask. **Is Ma . . . ?**

She's alive . . .

Rhodd let out a dry sob of relief. Her first thought had been that Ma must be dead – that Red would never have left her otherwise.

You shouldn't have left her – you should be with her! It was so much easier to share mind-shapes with Red than it was to talk.

She made me come after you, Red told her. **Last night, she suddenly sat up – called out your name. She told me to get Gar. She could see you trapped somewhere in the dark. And she sent us after you.**

A low growl. **The boy insisted on coming by the road**

173

even though I could smell that you had climbed the cliff. He said I'd never make it up those rocks at my age. A sniff.

I kept trying to tell him that if we went that way I couldn't tell where to start hunting for your scent. We were just wandering around in the dark. It was only because that rabbit found us on the road . . .

So the rabbit wasn't so stupid after all. Rhodd kept that thought to herself. *If it hadn't been for the rabbit, they might never have found me.* She didn't have the heart to say that to Red.

Gar's footsteps were returning. It sounded like he was dragging something heavy behind him.

'Watch out, Rhodd,' he grunted. 'Stand to the side. Out the way, Red.'

Rhodd pulled herself agonisingly to her feet. A night's sleep had reduced the pain enough for her to stand. She looked up as Gar lowered a thick branch down from above. It had plenty of side branches but it was bare of leaves. Some great tree must have shed this limb in its struggle to stay alive. But for Rhodd it would make a perfect ladder.

'You can use the side branches as steps,' Gar called down. 'Just take it slowly.'

Rhodd slung her bag on to her shoulder and put her foot on the lowest side branch, testing it to see that it would take her weight. She had to grit her teeth against the shifting and stabbing of her broken ribs as she reached to pull herself up. But she kept going, eyes fixed on the circle of sky which was bluing above her as the sun rose. Up and up . . .

The faces of Gar and Red swam into focus and then dissolved into a swimming blur. By the time her head reached the surface Rhodd was sobbing, but it was as much in relief that she was not going to die under the dark earth as from the pain.

Gar's strong hands were gripping her wrists, pulling her up into daylight, and Red's wet tongue was washing the earth and salty tear-tracks from her cheeks. Gar buried his dark head in her bright hair and wrapped his wiry arms around her and Rhodd yelped and then laughed and hugged him back. The hugging really hurt, but it was worth the pain.

'I thought . . . I thought . . .' They both knew what she had thought, that she would die down there, all alone, that she would never see Gar again, nor Red, nor . . . Rhodd looked up quickly, but the sky was empty. No falcon was hurtling from the clouds to make sure she was safe.

The gap in her soul where he should have been ached more than any of her physical pains.

Gar was talking. 'Got each other out of worse scrapes

than that, Rhodd.' He didn't trust himself to raise his head from the hug to look at her. His voice was muffled by her hair, but they both knew it wasn't true. All this was a lot more serious than the bullying of the Johnson brothers.

'You're safe now,' he told her.

CHAPTER 26

At last, Gar and Rhodd broke apart and he looked at her properly for the first time. His face blanched in shock before he could hide it. This was not the girl he had known like a sister since childhood.

The wild child that had walked out of the marsh was back.

Gone was Rhodd's long prim smock. Her undershirt hung in rags. Gar had never before seen the swirling scars on her legs which were glowing even through thick layers of dirt. He had never before seen her sun-bright mane stand up like a dark crown of feathers, untamed and stiffened with wind and rain and mud.

Rhodd stepped back when she saw Gar's face. She looked down and saw herself – this new Rhodd – through his eyes.

'What?' she demanded. 'Why are you . . . staring?' Her black eyes burned, savage. The rage she had always kept caged within her was closer to the surface now. She was poised like a bird ready for flight, ready for rejection. She would go on without him, if she must.

But Gar was grinning, that grin that was as old as their friendship. 'Reckon you could do with a good wash, Rhodd. What would your ma say, out without your nice smock!'

And Rhodd laughed and he laughed and their laughter drove away any doubt that all was well between them. Because Gar realised that he was seeing clearly for the first time what had always been there – the wild creature that had been disguised by Ma in her fight for Rhodd's survival.

'How is Ma?' Rhodd asked him quickly.

Gar paused. 'Weak,' he admitted. 'But we moved her to our house – my mam is looking after her.'

'And the otters?'

'Getting fat on goat's milk!' Gar grinned.

As they talked, the rabbit had been sitting a little apart, quietly getting on with washing its whiskers. Rhodd turned away from Gar and went to kneel beside it.

Thank you. You saved me.

The rabbit shrugged. **No more than you did for me.** It

was no longer the shivering creature in fear for its life.

How did you get out of that hole? she asked it.

The rabbit looked back at her as if she was stupid. **I dug. I dug a tunnel. That's what rabbits do.** Its role in Rhodd's rescue appeared to have given it a new confidence. In fact, it was almost too cocky.

But your paw?

You don't use your back paws for digging. Do you know nothing?

Rhodd was rapidly realising that she did know very little when it came to rabbits.

Couldn't get you out on my own, great overgrown lump like you, could I? So I went under the wall, found them two in the road. The rabbit pointed the tip of a long ear in the direction of Gar and Red. **Not too bright, the pair of them, are they? Reckon that lad's not got all his buttons on, he didn't understand anything I tried to tell him – but I persuaded the stupid dog to come with me in the end . . .**

Red growled a low growl but it wasn't the rabbit that was upsetting him.

Someone's coming, he warned Rhodd. His sharp ears had picked up the thud of horses' hooves. **They mean you harm. We need to go.**

Almost at the same moment Rhodd and Gar heard

shouts. As she had expected, the gamekeeper had brought help.

'He's . . . back!' Rhodd scrambled to her feet, clutching her ribs and wincing. She looked wildly about for an escape.

'Come on, Rhodd!' Gar seized her hand and pointed at the stone wall. 'We just need to get over the wall, they can't do anything to us if we're off Lord Stanley's land. That's what the law says.'

Rhodd wasn't at all sure about the protection of the law but all her instincts were telling her to run. The trouble was that her ribs were stabbing her with every breath. The rabbit sat paralysed, his nose twitching in terror. He was looking a lot less cocky now.

'Not leaving . . . rabbit,' Rhodd gasped. She pulled her hand free from Gar's grasp. She grabbed the rabbit and thrust him into her bag, swinging it up on to her shoulder. Then she wrapped her arms around her ribs, trying to hold her broken body together. 'Let's . . . go!'

She and Gar set off for the wall, Red on their heels. Two horses appeared over the brow of the slope, and on their backs, the gamekeeper – with his arm in a sling – and the upright, arrogant figure of Lord Stanley.

The gamekeeper's horse pulled up at the sight of them. It had not forgotten the name of Hafren. Lord Stanley lurched forward in the saddle as his own horse instinctively followed suit. It stopped so quickly it almost unseated its master, earning itself a curse and a savage kick.

And then Lord Stanley caught sight of Gar. He stopped kicking his horse and stared fixedly at the boy. Some emotion writhed beneath the smooth rubbery flesh. Rhodd could not tell what it was. But it looked like he was – for a moment – less sure about everything.

The gamekeeper gave his own horse a sharp kick with his spurs. 'Ride on!' But it refused to move.

Rhodd and Gar had reached the boundary to the estate. She knew it would take her time to scramble over that wall. She looked back at the gamekeeper's horse.

Please, give me time. Give me time to do Hafren's work, she begged it. **I have to find the river.**

The horse stood still. And no amount of spurring or cursing by the gamekeeper could shift it.

Lord Stanley raised his crop and slashed it against his horse's rump. 'Ride on,' he barked. Whatever it was that had made him pause a moment ago, he had obviously decided to ignore it.

Rhodd shifted her gaze to Lord Stanley's horse. **Please. Just give us time to get away.**

The horse stood as still as its companion, ignoring his

Lordship's furious whipping. Its ears twitched in irritation at the crop as if it was no more than an annoying fly. It did not shift.

Go, the horse told her. **We will not move.**

Rhodd's last view as Gar boosted her and then dragged her over the wall was the flabbergasted faces of the gamekeeper and Lord Stanley. They sat impotent and gaping open-mouthed with disbelief that their horses – so long broken to human will – were refusing to obey them.

Red bounded over the wall after Rhodd and Gar. They were safely off Lord Stanley's land at last.

CHAPTER 27

I'm starving. Where's the spinach?

It was the rabbit's voice, from her bag. And it reminded Rhodd of the practical reality that she couldn't remember when she had last eaten. She realised she was as hungry as the rabbit.

You ate it all, she told it. **And the apples. There's nothing left.**

A sniff from the bag. The rabbit was clearly unimpressed. **Let me out, then.**

On the other side of the wall was a wide track that must once have carried coaches to the village at the time when it was a busy port. It was now full of ruts and potholes; it was not worth anyone paying the upkeep for a road that went nowhere that anyone wanted to go.

She knew Gar was waiting for her to tell him what next. But she had no idea. Food seemed like a good plan.

Rhodd took the rabbit out and set it down. She turned to Gar. 'You got . . . food?' Her words were still halting, hesitant.

'Oh, yeah . . . I forgot.'

She scuffed him over the head, 'Nitwit!' and he gave her a shove back.

'Been a bit busy saving your life, Rhodd!'

The rabbit had lolloped off under a hedge into a field in the hope of finding grass, and the pair of them squeezed under the hedge after it, with Red following behind. They all felt safer off the road.

Gar opened his bag to show her what he'd brought. Hard-boiled eggs, cheese, and stuff from Bethan's vegetable patch. 'Reckon my ma gave us enough to feed an army.'

The rabbit returned – there was no grass in the scorched field – and the carrots were gone before Rhodd and Gar even had a bite.

Gar shifted uneasily as they sat eating in silence. He seemed to be finding it hard to know what to say. There was an awkwardness between them.

In the end, Gar's curiosity got the better of him. 'How did your ma know what had happened to you,

Rhodd? She told me you were trapped somewhere —
somewhere in the dark . . .'

Rhodd shrugged. 'She just knows stuff.'

Gar nodded. Even though he was passionate about
facts, growing up alongside Rhodd had taught him that
there were things that you couldn't learn from books.

He looked like he had more questions. But they had
eaten and it was time to move on. They picked up their
bags and returned to the road. The rabbit hopped unevenly
after them. It seemed to have learned to get around without
its lost foot.

Back at the road, the pair stopped. It was time to make
a decision. One way led back home. The other way led . . .
neither of them knew where. Gar looked at the newly
wilded Rhodd that stood beside him.

'Which way?' he asked. It had never been like this in the
past — in all their larks and adventures over the years they
had been equal partners. Everything was different now.

Rhodd said nothing. Her head moved in quick,
sudden turns. Her movements were as much animal as
human, her body quivering with senses that people had
forgotten. She was hearing things Gar could not hear,
smelling things he could not smell. One moment she took
on the stillness of a tree, rooted in the earth, the next she

moved with the flickering brilliance of a flame.

Red was whining anxiously.

'He wants to get back to your ma,' Gar said.

Rhodd nodded. 'I know.'

The air was full of invisible threads pulling each of them in different directions.

'I ought to go back to my ma too,' Gar said slowly. 'Lord Stanley is turning us all out of our homes tomorrow . . .'

He hesitated. 'Your ma told me you wouldn't be coming back with me.' A long pause, like it was hard to say the next bit. 'She said . . . she said I had to let you go.'

Rhodd could hear how Gar was being torn in two. He had always told her how he longed to get out of the village. To take the open road ahead and never look back. To find the life that was waiting for him. She knew that all his pent-up hunger for adventure was telling him to go with her. But duty was calling him back to his mother.

'Thing is, my ma needs me,' he finished.

I need you too, Rhodd thought but did not say. She felt so alone. She knew without looking that the sky was empty overhead, her falcon was not hovering over her. She had given up hoping for the quickening of joy that his wing-beats brought to her heart.

How could she bear to lose Gar again? But how could she ask him to come with her, when she understood so little of the task ahead?

'Rhodd! At least tell me where you are going!' Gar demanded finally. 'What's this all about?' As always, he needed to understand.

Rhodd turned to face him and her eyes were black, bottomless, burning with excitement.

'I can . . . smell . . . smell it, Gar.' Rhodd had almost forgotten how to speak in words. She was translating from her first language. The language of the wild.

'Smell what?'

'The . . . river. I can . . . smell . . . water.'

'The river's gone, Rhodd,' Gar told her flatly. 'The marsh took it.'

'No. It's over there. I know it is.' Rhodd pointed in the direction that would take them away from the village. Towards the hazy blue of the hills. 'I can't . . . go back, Gar. I have to . . . to find the river. That's what Ma said. Find the river . . . wash away . . . the marsh . . .' She spoke almost as if she was in a dream. 'Stop the Sickness.'

'What are you on about?' Gar's first instinct was to dismiss all this as fairy tales. But he'd been Rhodd's friend long enough to hesitate.

Rhodd continued, 'If the marsh is washed away . . . the river . . . will come back . . .'

Gar picked up the idea. 'And then the village will come back to life!' There was a new excitement in his voice. He could see the logic here. If he went with Rhodd, could he help to save the village? The village was his home in a way that it had never been hers.

'How could you do it? How could you bring the river back?' he demanded.

But these were questions that Rhodd could not answer. And she was already turning away, summoned by some call that Gar could not hear. Red pattered after her and pawed at her scarred legs.

I have to go back to her, Rhodd, he told her. **I can't help you any more.**

Rhodd sank to her knees, wincing at the pain in her ribs, and wrapped her arms around Red's thick neck. **I know.**

A long pause as she swallowed something in her throat. She pressed her forehead against his, in the old way she had done when he became her first friend outside the wild.

Tell Ma . . .

She understands, Rhodd. I don't need to tell her anything.

Rhodd nodded and smoothed away the wet stuff that

had dripped on to Red's fur. She stood up, after placing a final kiss on his forehead. The old dog turned and bounded away, old joints loosened by longing. He was desperate to be back at Ma's bedside, to keep her heart beating as long as he could.

Rhodd watched him go, then sighed and hoisted her bag on her shoulder. Everything – including Ma's life – depended on her. It was time to go. With or without Gar.

The rabbit was lolloping eagerly ahead of her. She knew it had smelled the water, just like she had.

Come on, slow coach! it called back to her. But then it stopped and sniffed the air. Rhodd went to kneel beside it.

What is it?

The rabbit was quivering just as it had in the trap when she first found it. This was real fear.

The river. It isn't a river. It smells . . . wrong . . . bad.

Rhodd shivered. She stood up and looked back in a final appeal to Gar. He still hadn't moved.

'Gar . . .' She was puzzled. Scared. 'The rabbit . . . it says . . . it says it is a river . . . but not a river.' She knew the rabbit was right. She could sense it too now. 'It smells wrong.'

Her eyes met Gar's, black eyes beseeching blue, and the yellow rims were brimming with tears. She knew she might have to do this alone, but . . .

'I don't understand, Gar. Help me.'

Rhodd was telling Gar that she needed him. Begging him to go with her. And without a backward glance – even though it made no sense – he chose his path. And followed her.

CHAPTER 28

Round the next corner, the road plunged dark into what they called a holloway in those parts. It was a sunken track worn deep into the earth by the footfalls and wagon wheels of centuries, before the village had been forgotten by the world.

The hedges reached up high from the deep banks, walling Rhodd and Gar in and shutting out the sky. The shadows were filled with gloom. Rhodd picked up the rabbit and held it close.

Don't be scared. But the truth was that the words of comfort were as much for her as they were for the rabbit. **I'll keep you safe.**

It snuffled. **Maybe.** It didn't seem to be the most optimistic of rabbits. But it nestled close, sensing Rhodd's need.

Over their heads there should have been a canopy of green foliage casting dappled sunlight and shade, but the branches above them were more like the arms of dying men clutching at one another in desperation. Their leaves had shrivelled and dropped and lay thick and dry and dusty as ashes underfoot. Without water, nothing could live.

'This is . . .' Rhodd searched her head. Words were becoming harder to find.

'Sad,' Gar finished the words for her.

Rhodd nodded. 'Sad.' That was it. A very little word it was, for this overwhelming feeling of emptiness, for the absence of . . . everything. The soaring joy of birdsong, the cries and rustles of creatures creeping about their everyday business of survival . . . *Where have they gone? Will they ever return?* she thought to herself. Had she woken up too late to save it all?

'Is this why you're here, Rhodd?' Gar's voice was soft, subdued in the half-light. 'To stop all this . . . death?'

Rhodd's pale face was taut, tense. The fear that she might fail flickered behind her eyes.

'Bring back . . . the river.' It was the only answer she could find to Gar's question and she repeated it softly, under her breath. 'Bring back . . . the river.' Trying to make herself believe. Ma's words were like a mantra, chanting in her brain. But it represented a quest so enormous and impossible that the words seemed to mean almost nothing. How to go about it – and what terrible price she might have to pay – all that was unseeable. Unsayable.

'Can you do it?' Gar's voice was still soft but the question was brutal.

Rhodd shrugged. 'Try.' It was all she could manage. Her whole body felt like a shrug, a shrug of fear and doubt.

She looked up at the brittle basket-weave above her head and stroked the rabbit's soft fur. More than ever Rhodd longed for a glimpse of her falcon, connecting her to the skies, showing her the way. Without him, all she could do was to follow the smell of water. And hope.

Without them noticing, the track was no longer sloping down but leading them steadily and secretly upwards, so that when they emerged at last from the holloway they both gasped at the scorch of the sun.

They were at the brow of a hill overlooking a deep valley.

Rhodd kept her eyes fixed on the empty sky. She dared not look down. This was the moment of truth, and she must face it without her falcon. She reached out for Gar's hand and he squeezed it.

But he was already looking down, and when she glanced over, she could see horror in his face.

Rhodd clenched her jaw and, at last, made herself look. There below her, straight as an arrow, was a strip of water that gleamed like burnished bronze in the midday sun. Rhodd had dreamed of seeing the river for so long. But this was not what she had longed for. There was nothing natural about this waterway.

It was accurate and straight as a ruler, walled in by brick and stone, with none of the merry twists and idle turns of a wild river. The water looked thick, stagnant; it was not flowing. This was a force of nature imprisoned.

'How can . . . ? That cannot . . . cannot be a . . . river?' Never had words tasted so wrong in Rhodd's mouth. She thought she might vomit. 'It is a . . . dead thing.'

CHAPTER 29

'Somebody's tried to turn it into a canal.' Gar's frown was furrowing those deep lines between his brows. His sharp eyes narrowed as he took it in. 'Look, Rhodd.'

Rhodd didn't want to keep looking. Her reaction to the imprisoned river was instinctive, emotional, outraged. She was overwhelmed by grief and fury.

Gar's reaction was to work out what had happened. What men had done here.

She followed his pointing finger.

'See – they've walled it in with stone – got rid of the bends to make it flow faster. I reckon they must have narrowed its mouth somewhere too, narrowed the channel from the sea . . .'

Rhodd could hardly breathe. It felt like her own mouth

had been blocked up, her own limbs had been bound so tight she could barely move.

You're hurting me! The rabbit gave a squeak of protest as, unconsciously, her hands tightened around its thin body. **Put me down.**

Sorry. She held its softness against her cheek for comfort – her own comfort – before she let it go. She put it down, facing away from what had once been the river. She didn't want to look, even though it was still there behind her.

The more Rhodd looked, the more she felt the agony of the crippled river. Nothing was right about this water. She knew in her soul that old rivers meander slow and steady to the sea. They take their sweet time, carving out wide bends, calming the bubbling energy of the mountain streams that made them. Ebbing and flowing with the tides. Until with a gentle sigh of surrender they lose themselves in the salty oceans.

But all that wild beauty had been tamed and tortured into the straight waterway that lay below them.

The rabbit looked down from the hill and saw what she saw. It slumped in misery. **It's dead. All dead.**

Gar was still working it out. He pointed again. 'Look, Rhodd – they've built a lock down there . . .' He sounded almost excited. He'd read about engineering like this in the schoolmaster's books, but he'd never seen it.

All Rhodd could see was a huge black box built like a cage in the water. 'Lock' sounded about right. She knew that you needed locks for a prison.

'But why . . .' Rhodd was gasping for air. 'What's it all for?'

Gar's quick brain was whirring, working out the whats and the whys for himself. 'Whoever did it wanted to control the water . . . change the route of the river to make it quicker, make the ships sail faster. Make more money.'

Ma had never had much truck with money. They'd never had any, for one thing. Most of what they ate, they had bartered for something else. She knew what Ma would have called this. 'Greed, then,' Rhodd said flatly.

Greed was one of the words Rhodd had always struggled with. Creatures did not have a shape for that word. Why kill if you did not need food? Why eat when you weren't hungry? Why take more of something if you didn't need it?

Gar nodded. He was looking less excited now. His mind was flying beyond the man-made canal, back to the marsh and the village. And his excitement was being replaced by an anger of his own.

'It's not worked though, Rhodd.'

Rhodd was beyond being able to understand what Gar was on about. So she said nothing, waited for him to explain.

'There are no ships. The river – canal – whatever you call it . . . it's empty. If this is where all the ships were supposed to go – the ones that used to come to our village – then where are they?'

CHAPTER 30

The last place Rhodd wanted to go was closer to the river – or what was left of it. But it seemed like the only logical place to go.

Without a word, she and Gar linked hands and slipped and slithered down the hillside to the water's edge. Her broken ribs were like knives jabbing into her side. The rabbit looked dubious, but limped slowly after them.

The water smelled stagnant, sluggish. It barely moved. Thick clouds of flies hovered over it, the only life to be seen. The place was deserted.

Gar pointed to some machines with long necks hanging over the banks. 'Ma said they used to have things like that on the quayside back home, before the river disappeared,' he told Rhodd.

A voice came from behind them. 'Cranes, that's what he called 'em.' A man, skinny as a corpse, had emerged from a small cottage next to the lock.

Rhodd darted behind Gar, like a wary animal. Remembered the fear in the gamekeeper's face, and the sign he had made when he saw her – the sign to ward off evil. She didn't want to see that look on anybody's face again. But with only the last shreds of her undershirt clinging to her scarred body, she could no longer hide her wildness. She was no longer at home in this human world – she had shuffled it off like an extra skin.

The man rubbed his eyes as if their voices had woken him from a long sleep. 'Cranes,' he said again. 'To unload all them ships. Ha!'

A bitter laugh got stuck in his throat and he coughed it up and spat it into the water. 'All them ships he promised us, them ships that never came. This was supposed to be the new quayside here, so they could unload closer to the city over there.' He nodded his head towards the east. 'He said it would bring the railway here, bring more jobs, more money.'

None of the words he was speaking made sense to Rhodd. *City, railway, jobs, money.* She was watching the gobbet of spit floating, still, on the surface of the water.

There was no current to carry it away.

Gar stepped closer to the man. There was stuff he needed to know.

'Who's "he"?' Gar demanded quickly. 'Who was it that promised the ships would come here?'

'His Lordship – from that big house up there.' The man nodded up the hill. His skin had an unhealthy, slightly greenish tinge, as if he had been living under a stone.

He looks like a newt, Rhodd thought idly. She looked around for the rabbit, but it had disappeared.

Gar had gone very pale. 'Lord Stanley?' It sounded like the name had got stuck like gristle between his gritted teeth.

'Is that his name? Mebbe.' The man shrugged and then coughed and spat again.

Rhodd wondered how long the man had been living there, spitting into the river. *More spit in there than fresh water*, she thought. She stared despairingly out over the dead river. She wasn't interested in all this talk about cranes and ships. *How can I ever make this water flow free again?* she thought.

But now he'd got started, newt-man couldn't stop talking. He seemed to have a whole chestful of bitterness to cough up. 'Young fool, he was, whatever his fancy title.

Wanted faster ships, bigger ships, didn't he? The river weren't flowing fast enough for him, it weren't deep enough for him. The old village weren't making enough money to pay for his fancy house an' his fancy horses.'

Another bitter phlegm-filled laugh. 'Brought hundreds of men here, he did, from all over. Paid 'em in pennies – got 'em to dig a new bed for the river. Wanted it to do his bidding . . .'

Rhodd saw Gar's fists clench at his sides. He didn't seem to have any words. So Rhodd plucked up her courage and asked the next question for him. 'And did it? Did the river do his bidding?' It seemed a strange thing to ask a river to do.

''Course not. 'Acos the marsh came, didn't it?'

Rhodd whispered. 'The marsh swallowed the river.'

The man nodded then jerked his head sideways, towards the west. 'The marsh spread and spread, an' choked the water off from the sea. Blocked his new channel with mud. So this bit here is all that's left.'

He paused. 'It weren't natural, the way the marsh spread so fast.' His voice dropped to a whisper. 'They say there's summat out there . . .'

The man's face changed suddenly. He was staring at Rhodd. 'You're that . . . that . . .' He didn't know what to call her, so he gave up. 'What came out of there, out o' the marsh . . .' He crossed himself. His eyes were fixed on her scarred limbs.

Gar stepped back in front of Rhodd. He wanted more facts. 'So that's why the river stopped flowing?' he insisted. 'Lord Stanley had the canal made – and then the marsh came?'

'Yeah. An' now he's trying to sell it.' The man was backing away, peering round Gar at Rhodd. As he went, he pointed to a sign on the side of the cottage.

The sign looked just like the one that Lord Stanley's man had posted on the pub, back in the village. Gar read it out loud. 'River and lock-keeper's house for sale. Apply to' – his mouth screwed up at the name – 'Lord Stanley.'

'Got to be gone by tomorrow, His Lordship says. Me, I'll be glad to see the back of this place.'

A final spit, and the lock-keeper disappeared inside.

'My father.' The words were choking Gar. 'Lord Stanley. He destroyed the river. Destroyed all our lives. It is him that has killed everything, Rhodd. And his rotten blood is running in my veins.'

He was shaking, clawed at himself as if he wanted to flay his own skin. 'My father did this.'

Rhodd tried to wrap her arms around him, tried to contain his anger. 'Not your fault, Gar,' she whispered. She realised now what Lord Stanley had been lying about. This was the great lie that she had seen slithering like an eel across his face. He knew exactly why the river had deserted the town – because *he* had caused it. 'It's not your fault,' she said again. 'And we are going to bring the river back. That's why—'

Gar wasn't listening. He pulled away from her in a fury. 'It's no good, Rhodd. It's too late.' She had never seen him like this. All his normal calm logic and reason were gone.

'It's not too late, Ma told me to—' Rhodd started.

'What – that rubbish about the river? That's all just witchcraft!'

Rhodd winced at the word 'witchcraft', but Gar did not stop. 'That's all it is – fairy tales! It's not real, Rhodd!' All his anger was turned on her now. He stepped back, glaring at her, teeth bared. 'What *is* real is that tomorrow my ma – and your ma – will have nowhere to live. But you never cared about that anyway, did you?'

Gar stormed away, though he didn't get far. There was nowhere for him to go. Rhodd watched him sinking to the ground to sob, his head in his hands. She went over and kneeled beside him but every time she tried to give him a hug, he pushed her away.

The rabbit hopped over, dandelion petals dangling from its whiskers. It had been busy raiding the lock-keeper's weedy patch of garden. Its nose twitched in puzzlement. **Is he hungry?** It didn't seem to understand much apart from hunger.

No, he's sad, Rhodd told it. **Like when your mother went away.**

The rabbit burrowed its way on to Gar's lap, and his hand sneaked out to stroke it. Gradually his body stopped shaking and his sobs subsided and he slept, exhausted. The sun was setting in the west, and the stagnant water glowed red as a bloody scar in front of Rhodd as she kneeled beside Gar. She shivered. Tomorrow was eviction day. And Gar was wrong, she did care. This was Ma's last night before she lost her home. Ma, who had taken her in and given her shelter, kept her safe for so long.

In a fury, Rhodd dug her nails deep into the dry earth, crushed it into fistfuls between her fingers. When she opened her hands, it trickled away like dust. There was no goodness left in this soil.

'Dust to dust, ashes to ashes,' Rhodd muttered. She'd

heard the priest chanting those words over the dead, as they were buried in their graves.

She had to do something to bring life back to this place, although she still had no idea what. It was too big for her, this thing. She still understood so little of what had happened. But in her guts she knew this wasn't just the work of one greedy man. There was something else that had wreaked this devastation and it was waiting for her, out on the marsh.

She looked up at the sky. It was crimson . . . angry . . . empty. She had given up hope of seeing her Peregrine and ever again feeling her heart soar with his. It was her own fault. She had hidden away for too long and now she had to do this alone.

Still kneeling, Rhodd reached her arms to the sky. For anyone watching it would have been impossible to tell whether this scarred and ragged creature was praying – or preparing to fly. Perhaps for her, they were the same thing.

Let me see.

She no longer dared to let herself hope that her falcon was still hovering beyond her sight, but she remembered the voice that had urged her up the cliff. She needed its help now.

Show me. I am ready to look.

The name of Hafren was quivering on her lips. She fixed her dark eyes on the burning arrow of the river, pointing the way out to the west where it had once flowed free to the sea. And for the first time in her life, she felt her spirit rise from her body and soar to the sky.

'Further, further,' Rhodd muttered under her breath.

She did not understand what power was helping her. Released to roam under the sky, her spirit flew with the freedom of her falcon – though her falcon was still nowhere to be seen.

The body Rhodd had left behind, kneeling on the earth next to Gar, shuddered and trembled. Her human heart was beating fast, fluttering in her broken rib cage. There was danger in this.

A cold, dank stench rose up towards her spirit as it flew to the edge of the marsh, like clammy clutching fingers. There was a stink of poison. It was the poison that had brought the Sickness, the poison that was killing birds, otters, everything that lived.

Below lay something terrible. It was the stuff of nightmares. Something was trying to snatch her spirit down, to swallow it into its own darkness, just as it had swallowed the river, just as it had swallowed those boys. What creature could be the source of such evil?

Her spirit flew higher, higher, skimming over the marsh. Rhodd would have to face whatever lay down there tomorrow.

Back by the riverbank, darkness had fallen around Rhodd's abandoned body. Her heart was harkening to a language in which the unseen world was as real as the seen. Her head was still as a falcon's head when it sights its prey.

'Beyond, beyond!' she was muttering. She needed her spirit to find for her the hope that something lay beyond the marsh. Something worth fighting for.

The name of Hafren took shape in Rhodd's mind.

Help me to see! Her spirit, flying on alone, was fixed on the mystery of an other-where, an other-land.

And at last, there it was. Rhodd gasped.

She heard a wild river tumbling, rushing, unstoppable, to greet the sea. She smelled a wide ocean, stretching to infinite horizons beyond.

Was it memory? Was it witchcraft, like Gar had said? Or was her spirit showing her the possibility of what *could be* once again, of what the future might hold, if only Rhodd had the courage to make it happen?

And then came that voice. And she knew it for Hafren's voice.

I will help you.

Rhodd's spirit flew back to her body.

She furled her arms around her aching ribs and lay on the ground next to Gar, exhausted. The yellow rims of her eyes slid shut.

She had a promise.

It was the distant sound of wind and water on waves that soothed Rhodd to sleep that night. An ancient lullaby. The tang of salt was on her lips and for the first time in her memory, she could smell the sea.

Step back into the wild-ness, child,

Where no man goes.

And face the fight of your life.

It is time to win back the wild world.

CHAPTER 31

Rhodd woke to moonlight and the certain knowledge that Gar was gone.

A full moon was high in the sky. She had felt the pull and push of it on her body as she slept, like its pull and push on the waters of the earth. It was on nights like this that the boys of the village had been lured out to the marsh. And she knew without a doubt, that was where Gar had gone too.

'No, Gar!' Rhodd cried out after him, into the night. 'Gar!'

But there was no answering shout.

'No, not on your own, Gar!'

She struggled fast to her feet, dislodging the rabbit from where it had curled warm against her body. Her head was still heavy with moon dreams. A distant lonely church bell chimed a single note. One hour past midnight. She couldn't tell when Gar had left, nor how much of a head start he had. But she wouldn't leave him to face what was out there alone. Even if he was past caring what happened to him.

She knew it was a darkness – the darkness of despair – inside Gar that had driven him out into the marsh. Darkness seeking darkness. *My father did this.* It was almost the last thing he'd said to Rhodd. His father's guilt weighed as heavy on him as if it was his own. Today was the day of the evictions. With no school and no home, Gar had no future. Nothing to live for.

Stay here, she told the rabbit. **There's food for you in that garden. The newt-man won't bother you. He's leaving anyway.** She picked the creature up and nuzzled her nose against his. **Thank you. You saved me from that hole.**

The rabbit sneezed and rubbed its whiskers. **We saved each other.** It might have been blushing beneath its fur. **Anyway, I'm hungry.** It hopped off with its lopsided hop to find what was left of those dandelions.

Well, at least I've kept one rabbit alive, Rhodd thought grimly. It wasn't much, when everything around her was dead or dying. But the rabbit had reminded her that she was hungry too.

Never start the day without breakfast, Rhodd! Ma's voice was in her head again.

Even if it's the middle of the night, Ma? It almost had the comfort of a conversation.

Rhodd patted her bag. It was empty, but Gar had left his bag behind and his was still half-full. He'd taken nothing.

Reckon he thought he'd have no need for food, where he's planning to go, thought Rhodd. *I need to find him before* . . . But she didn't want to think about what Gar might be already facing out there, so she stuffed a couple of hard-boiled eggs into her mouth and ran.

Faster, faster, she urged her legs. There was no doubt which way she was heading. The straight waterway shone ahead of her, silvered in the moonlight. It was the finger of a ghost, pointing the way back to the marsh, back to the wild-ness she had escaped all those years ago. Before she was old enough to fight.

It was anger that kept Rhodd running through that night, in spite of the pain from her ribs. Anger and fear – for Gar, for Ma, for the whole wild world that was dead or dying around her.

Beside her, the sight of the dead river hurt like a knife-blade cutting into her skin. 'Water cannot be tamed . . .' Rhodd was muttering. 'Water can be ruled by nothing but the moon and the sun . . .' These were truths that nobody had needed to teach Rhodd in a schoolroom. These were the truths she had always known.

She found herself trying to speak to the old river as she had always spoken to the creatures of the earth, as she had learned to speak to the trees.

You will run free. She pounded out the promise with her bare feet on the riverbank, pounded it out with her heartbeats. **You will run free.**

There was no answer. There was only silence.

That night felt like the longest night of Rhodd's life, as the moon sank slowly towards an unseen horizon. She kept telling herself this way was quicker than her weary trudge over the hills. Her spirit-flight the night before had showed her that this man-made channel would take her in a straight line, back to the marsh. She had gone full circle, back to where all this had started.

Rhodd's breath kept catching in her chest – like a caged and frightened bird – when she remembered the lost children, Ma's son Rhys amongst them.

They never came back, she reminded herself. What if

Gar never came back? What horrors might he be facing already, before she could reach him?

'Run faster, Rhodd!' she panted.

At last, pink fingers of dawn poked holes in the blue-black sky. The sun was rising in the east behind her, she could feel it through the rags of her undershirt.

The sun always rises, Rhodd. The words came as a whisper of love from wherever Ma lay, sick or . . .

'No, not dead. She is not dead! I still have time . . .'

Rhodd slowed to a halt and bent, gasping to get her breath. All around her light was creeping back to the earth. But it took courage to look up and see.

She raised her head, slowly, slowly.

And looked.

Before her lay the dark expanse of the marsh, emerging from the night. Somewhere on the far edge of it lay the village. The wilderness was shrouded in thick morning mist, but she levelled her eyes on it and this time she refused to look away.

'This time I will face you,' Rhodd vowed. The battle scars were burning on her bare legs.

Without a backwards glance, Rhodd walked out once again into the place where people did not go.

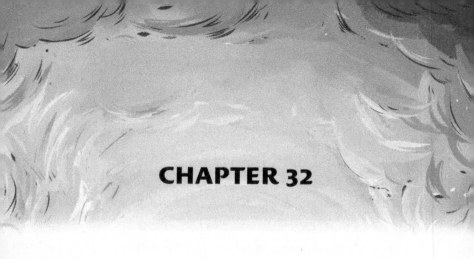

CHAPTER 32

The sky had never looked so big. It was as big as the fear inside her. Grey clouds were rising like mountains from the grey mudflats and blotting out the promise of the early sun.

Rhodd felt very alone as she stepped on to the marsh. She knew about the treachery of this place. Earth could become water from one footstep to the next. It was a place of deception and shifting sands and there was no mapping its deep channels on any man-made charts. 'Here today, gone tomorrow,' they'd always said back in the village, shaking their heads. 'There is no trusting the marsh . . .'

A stink rose to her nostrils, the revolting stench of . . . what? Was it just rotting mud and stagnant water? Or something else? There was no wind but Rhodd sensed that the stench was coming in regular waves. Was there something . . . something breathing out there? Was this the poisonous breath that had carried the Sickness to the village?

In the thin dawn light, dead reeds stood white as a forest of bones. They reminded Rhodd of the lost children – of Rhys and now Gar. 'No! You shall not have him!' she shouted, shivering away the image of a black reptilian tongue licking Gar's bones clean.

'Faster, faster!' she told herself. But she was having to watch her every step. Any bright patch of grass might conceal quicksand, which would suck her down and swallow her in moments.

Sharp pain surged through the old bites and stings on her legs. Something wanted to remind her of how much it had once hurt her – and could hurt her again.

'I do not fear you.' Rhodd said it out loud, just to hear herself say it. It was like trying out the truth. The wobble in the words made it sound less than convincing, and the soft sigh that whistled through the reeds might have been a sneer of mockery.

Rhodd stopped and peered into the distance. How far ahead of her could Gar be? Was she already too late?

Oh, where are you? Forgive me, come back to me! She glanced briefly up to the sky for comfort. She had never needed her falcon more. Her heart ached for him. But nothing moved there. The heavy, heaven-high clouds were still. The wind was holding its breath. The whole wild world was waiting.

'I need your eyes,' she cried out loud to whatever might hear her. And then the cry caught in her throat and fluttered there. Because there was a blur at the edge of her vision, a tremor that might have been wings, a quickening of the air.

She dared not look at it, lest she had imagined it.

Please . . . she begged. **Show me Gar.**

Rhodd lowered her eyes carefully, fixed them on the marsh ahead of her.

And then, with a gasp, she saw once more – for a few short moments – through her Peregrine's eyes.

'Gar!' There he was, in the distance, beyond her own seeing. It was Gar's slight, determined figure, walking fast away from her. He was still alive.

Thank you. Rhodd had a flicker of hope now that her falcon was hearing her. But the slight sliver of joy disappeared as she lost his eyes again. And was quickly replaced by dread.

There was something about the way Gar had been walking across the marsh – so much faster than she was daring to walk herself – that terrified her. His head was held high – he wasn't looking down to check for the deep gullies – and yet his feet never strayed from a safe path. His eyes were fixed on something.

'It is calling him,' Rhodd whispered. Gar was being *guided* by something through the marsh. Being lured on, into the heart of darkness.

Reckless now with fear, Rhodd set off at a run, clutching her ribs. The nagging ache of the broken bones was exhausting, but she could not stop. Looking down made her slower, and she was still trying to make out Gar in the distance. Her feet slid treacherously close to the edges of the gullies. She slipped, went in up to her thighs. The mud sucked at her legs, trying to pull her deeper. It felt like a living creature. And she was its prey.

Rhodd cursed one of the worst curses she'd picked up from the fishermen, back in the village. 'Let me go!' She dragged her legs out, panting.

In moments she was back on her feet and running. 'You can't stop!' she scolded herself. She was gaining on Gar – she could just see him with her own eyes now.

'Gar!' she shouted, but his head did not turn. He was being drawn deeper into the dark centre of the marsh. He walked as if he was mesmerised by whatever he could see in front of him.

Rhodd desperately tried to keep him in view whilst avoiding another slip into a gully. Solid earth became water under her feet, mere moments after Gar had safely passed. The channels shifted beneath Rhodd's feet as if there was indeed a living thing slithering in the silt, controlling the shape of the marsh. Gripping it in its coils.

The next time Rhodd slipped, she went right in. And when she opened her mouth to scream 'No!', the waters closed over her head and filled her lungs.

Rhodd had no memory of learning to swim. Nobody in the village – apart from Rhys's pa – had ever taught their children how to swim. It was an old fishermen's tradition – if the sea took you, the sea owned you. And no man must argue with the will of the sea.

But Rhodd was no child of that village. Her instincts for survival were the instincts of an animal, and they ran deep. Her feet flailed in the water and her hands struggled to free themselves from the weeds that were grabbing at her body. She fought against the weight of the water and for a moment her mouth found the air. She gasped it in.

But after that one deep gasp she was pulled down again . . . down and down. This wasn't just water. It was something else. Something . . . alive.

No! You will not take me! Rhodd did not know what

creature she was shouting her defiance at – but she knew something was sucking her in. Something wanted to stop her reaching Gar. Something wanted her dead.

Rhodd made herself open her eyes but she could see nothing through the murk. She was going to die down here, without air, without light.

Help me! She sent out a final plea to any creature that might be clinging to life in that wasteland. Anything that might help her.

And, like a miracle, there was an answering splash at the surface. A lithe shape slipped through the thick water and shimmered past her, down into the murky depths.

Push down on me. There was a nudge from below. Rhodd felt smooth fur pressing against her feet. Strong muscle rippled beneath the fur, and a powerful body was lifting her up towards the air.

Let me see! Let me use your eyes! Rhodd reached out in her mind to speak to it. The creature's eyes became hers, and she peered through the gloom and saw the side of the gully. It was just out of reach. But Rhodd had hope now.

She kicked hard and felt the slimy bank. Her toes and fingers became claws and she dug them deep into the mud and dragged herself up, one slow painful pull at a time.

At last, Rhodd's head broke above the water, and she

hung there, coughing out water that was thick with filth. A sleek whiskered head surfaced beside her.

It's you. Rhodd recognised the otter that had entrusted her with its pups. **Thank you.**

Are they safe? their mother demanded.

Safe – and growing fat, Rhodd replied.

The otter nodded. **Now you must complete your task. And bring the river back.**

Before Rhodd could thank it, it slid away into the reeds. The stench of fear lingered in the air behind it. No creature that had clung on to life here dared show itself for long.

With a great wrench of her muscles – agony for her ribs – Rhodd pulled herself over the bank and crawled on to drier ground. She lay there, exhausted. She had lost so much time. And Gar was still walking steadily on towards his fate.

CHAPTER 33

Get up! You cannot rest now.

Rhodd lifted her head. A rotting tree-stump rose from the flat wasteland, just a few feet from the gully.

And there, perched on the stump, was her falcon. He had been preening his chest feathers but now he raised his head and looked at her. It seemed as if he had been waiting for her there for ever.

She had never seen her falcon up close. His beak was a scimitar, curved to rip, to gut, to kill; his talons were daggers to pierce flesh, to deal out instant death. The black eyes of a murderer glinted against the brilliant yellow of the rims; his moustachioed face was all fierceness and fire. It seemed that the only softness about this creature was the tawny crop of feathers beneath his beak, but as Rhodd stood up she saw that each white feather on his chest was painted with a perfect black heart.

I need your help. Rhodd dared to take a step closer. Every bit of her yearned to touch him, to hold him, but she knew that was something she could never do. It had to be enough that he had come back to her.

I know, came the reply.

There was a long moment as their black eyes met, a moment when it seemed that he too was yearning for closeness. But then, with a few long lazy flaps of his great wings, his body rose and was at one with the air once more. From below, his wings were striped like a tiger, black against white, but as he soared and seized the wind, his upper wings were the blue of a summer sky.

It was so long since Rhodd had been able to see through her falcon's eyes. She had almost forgotten the sheer joy of it, forgotten her deep envy for the wind beneath his wings.

But she had never allowed him to show her the marsh before. Nor the dark truth that lay at the heart of it.

This is your task! Now face it! The shape of his thoughts floated down to her as he wheeled over the wild-ness.

And finally, she looked.

The desolate expanse of wasteland lay beneath her. She had always thought of this place as stagnant – dead – but from above it was clear to her now that it was *alive*; the channels were constantly shifting and rippling. There was a pattern here, carved out by the writhing of great coils. The falcon's eyes were showing her what she had always known in her heart. A living thing held this place in its fearsome, jealous grip.

A rumble shook the marsh. Black clouds were lowering ominously over the flat wastes, but Rhodd knew this time it wasn't thunder. It was the anger of a creature gathering itself for a kill.

Rhodd felt very cold.

Show me Gar.

What she saw through her falcon's eyes sent Rhodd tearing across the marsh. She did not look down for a moment. She had to trust the falcon's eyes to guide her and to keep her safe. Because Gar was no longer walking. His body was lying motionless on the mudflats.

It is time to decide

Whether to be hunter or hunted.

Will you be Peregrine?

Or prey?

CHAPTER 34

'*Airk . . . Airk . . .*'

A sharp falcon's cry hissed from Rhodd's mouth. She was crouched over Gar, shoulders hunched, and her arms encircled his limp body.

'You shall not have him . . .' she panted.

She was shielding the exhausted boy as a falcon protects its prey from predators, mantling it with its wide wings. Every bit of her body hurt – her broken ribs, her burning lungs and the scars of the swirling bites and stings on her legs. But she did not shift.

She was waiting for the beast to show itself. She could feel the rumble of its anger beneath her feet, could smell its stinking breath on her skin. It was close. It was everywhere. But she could not yet tell where.

Above her she knew her falcon was hovering, watching over her as it had done for so long. She saw the whole wide expanse of devastation with its eyes. But this had to be her battle alone now, the battle from which she had fled once before.

'I remember this place,' Rhodd whispered to herself. The sweet earth had been her playground then . . . the creatures of the wild world had been her playmates. A child born from a deep magic, ageless and unseen by human eye, left to wander free beneath the gaze of an ever-watchful guardian, her falcon. But it was a playground of innocent delights that had become a place of terror.

Here at the centre of the marsh was the beast's heartland, its lair. Everywhere its foul spawn – its offspring – were seething in the gullies. The mud sighed as the coils shifted and tightened around it. Rhodd could sense the creature's fury building. She was blocking the path to its prey.

Others had not escaped. There were white bones everywhere. Bones that Rhodd did not want to look at too closely. It was clear now that those lost children had not drowned. They had been fodder for this beast. It had lured them out here when the full moon and the spring tides had made it restless and stirred it from its sleep.

Were Rhys's bones lying here, with Why-Why's and

the rest? She thought of Ma's face waiting, steadfast, at the window for her son to walk home. *Maybe he'll come back one day, Rhodd* . . . Rhodd shook the memory away. She couldn't bear to remember the longing in Ma's eyes.

At least Gar was still alive. When she bent close, she could hear him muttering to himself as if he was in the clutches of a bad dream, 'My father . . . Not my . . .'

'It's all right, Gar. I'm here,' she whispered.

But then the bad dream became a living nightmare for both of them.

A thing of darkness slowly lifted its hideous flat head up from the marsh. Malevolent yellow eyes, split by a dark crack of pupil, were fixed on Rhodd, level with her own eyes but large as wagon wheels. It stared for a long moment. And then the grim line that was its mouth gaped open, and a black tongue forked and flickered out between dripping fangs. Tasting the air between them.

Rhodd shuddered and her scars stung as if those fangs were piercing her skin once more. *This* was the thing she had refused to see for so long. The thing that had driven her from the wild. But she did not flinch from her mantling crouch over Gar. She was Peregrine, defending her own.

'What are you?' she whispered. This creature was of the wild world, but there was nothing natural about what it had turned into. Whatever it might once have been, it had brooded and fed on its anger over the loss of the river until it had grown into this . . . this horror. It had bound the wild-ness in its coils until it had suffocated the thing it loved.

Gar stirred beneath Rhodd's body. He opened his eyes and peered round her and his face filled with horror. 'What is that, Rhodd?'

'Keep still,' Rhodd muttered. She was trying to work out what the creature was going to do. Waiting for its attack. In the wild you had to kill or be killed. Predator or prey. But in spite of her savage heart, Rhodd had never killed a living creature.

She kept her eyes fixed on the beast's eyes, which glittered between dull greenish scales. Its head was still held low and she could only guess at its real size. She was watching for its next move.

'It is the beast that stole the river,' she whispered to Gar.

'My father stole the river,' Gar flared back.

This really is no time to argue, Gar, thought Rhodd impatiently. But she knew Gar wouldn't let it go until he understood. 'Yes – your father stole the river from the village and walled it up in that canal thing. But then this creature took the river back from him . . .'

'How?' Even now, face to face with this monster, Gar still wanted answers.

'It stopped the water from flowing. It wrapped its coils between his canal and the sea – and made the marsh.'

'Why did it do that?'

'Will you ever stop asking questions?' hissed Rhodd, exasperated. 'Because it was angry, you nitwit!'

'Still not too happy, by the looks of things,' Gar murmured. The creature's cold eyes were fixed on Rhodd's eyes.

'For goodness' sake, shut up a minute,' snapped Rhodd. 'I need to . . .' All the time she spent talking to Gar, she was losing her focus on the beast.

'Are you trying to talk to it?' demanded Gar in disbelief. Despite his terror – or maybe because of it – a giggle slipped out. 'Reckon that thing's not here for a chat, Rhodd . . .' Even with the little that Gar understood about Rhodd's powers, the idea of having a conversation with this beast seemed plainly ridiculous.

The flat head began to sway slowly from side to side. Rhodd sensed that this was how it hypnotised its prey – this was how it had held those poor children frozen with fear before it attacked. Rhodd could feel the shifting of its immense coils as it gathered itself to strike.

'Hush!' she hissed at Gar. Her urgency silenced him for a moment. Rhodd was trying to think back to the time before she had left the wild, when she had spoken to the creatures of earth and air as easy as thinking. But she could not even tell what this creature was – and in any case, she sensed it spoke another language, a language that perhaps she had never learned.

How can I understand you? The mind-shapes in this beast's head were more ancient than those of any creature Rhodd had ever met. Its language came from a time when creatures dwelled in the depths of the oceans, before they crawled out and on to the earth.

'But I spoke to the trees . . .' Rhodd argued with herself out loud. Gar stared at her as if she had lost her mind.

'What? Don't be daft, Rhodd! How did you talk to trees?'

'Shut up, will you, Gar? Do you want to end up like that lot?'

Gar noticed the scattered piles of bones that she was nodding at and went very white. And, finally, kept quiet.

Rhodd did not relax her relentless focus. The beast tossed its huge head uneasily like it was trying to shake her off. But it did not rise up to strike. For the moment she had distracted it from devouring them.

Slowly, slowly, she was starting to understand it. To break through. She made the shapes in her head simple. This creature's thoughts were primeval. It knew nothing but cold and hot, hunger and killing, right and wrong. Perhaps love and loss – because she sensed that it had loved the river. And, certainly, rage.

You are angry.

Rhodd winced as she felt a great surge of fury flow through the beast's mind. She cowered, bowed her head, waiting for the strike. But she did not shift from her mantling crouch over Gar. She had to keep her friend safe.

Gar stared up at her in terror. He had felt her flinch; he guessed that she was bracing herself for an attack. She tried to grin at him reassuringly but it came out more as a grimace.

Still nothing happened. Rhodd lifted her head to look. The beast was tossing and turning its head. She could tell it was hesitating. It did not like her intrusion into its thoughts. In the lonely hell it had created for itself, it was a long time since it had communed with any other creature.

She delved back into its mind. It was a dark place. But she recognised the anger that twisted its thought-shapes. It was the same anger she had felt all her life. The same anger that had twisted Ma's lovely face when she spoke about the lost river.

She took a breath and tried again. **I am angry too,** she told it.

The beast lowered its hideous head a little, flat against the mud. It seemed to be listening. But there was a terrifying force boiling in its belly. Waiting to be unleashed . . .

A memory popped into Rhodd's head. A conversation with Gar. *Can you make animals do anything you want, Rhodd?*

Can I control them, do you mean? she'd snarled back at him. She'd barely been able to contain her fury with him at the time. *They aren't my toys . . . We are made of the same stuff, made of the same earth and the same water and the same air . . . the same fire!*

She saw the truth of her own words now. She and this creature were created from the same elements. They burned with the same anger for the loss of the wild world. She remembered how she had longed to unleash some mighty beast on the village to avenge those poor dead birds, to avenge the wild world. And now she had the chance.

The memory was growing into an idea. She saw what she must do.

She did not need to kill this thing. She had to harness its rage. Use it to wash away the marsh it had created around itself and to bring back the river.

But first she had to save Gar – and Ma. Before anything else, she had to attend to the people she had grown to love.

'Gar,' she said softly. These were human words, words the creature could not follow. 'You need to go back to the village. You need to run, faster than you have ever run. My falcon will be your guide through the marsh. He will show you the safe paths. Follow him.

'And then you need to warn them – Ma and Bethan and Red . . . and the rest of the village if you want – and get them to the top of the cliff as fast as you can. I don't know how long I can hold back this creature's anger.'

'But Rhodd – what about you? I can't leave you!'

'You have to leave me, Gar. This is what I am for. To save the river.'

'But Rhodd – we've always done everything together . . . all our lives!' He stopped. They both knew that this time was different. This was no lark like letting out Ma Johnson's pig. This was life . . . or death. Not just for them. For everyone. Everything.

'Go, Gar! No more questions!' Gar quailed at the savagery in Rhodd's black eyes. He nodded.

'Now – get up quickly, the moment I get up. And don't look back. Just run!'

Rhodd stood up and Gar stood up behind her. She was still shielding him with her body.

The beast quivered, but it kept its head low and did not strike. Rhodd locked its cold yellow eyes with hers.

Let him go. You can have me. I escaped you once. This time I will stay.

Would it understand a bargain? Her life in return for Gar's?

The beast sighed. Rhodd sensed a great weariness in it. But there was no promise in reply. Would it let Gar go? She had to take the chance.

'Tell Ma . . . tell her I love her.' Rhodd had her back to Gar and she was glad he could not see her wet face. She was struggling to speak.

'Cerys told me I must let you go, when the time came.' Gar's voice was shaking. He wailed, 'But I don't want to let you go, Rhodd!'

Rhodd nodded but she did not turn to look at Gar. Inside she was wailing too. She did not – and yet she did, with all her heart – want to see his dear face. One last time.

'Who are you, Rhodd?' Gar whispered. It was time for both of them finally to face the truth.

Rhodd shook her head. She shrugged. Dared not look back. 'Your friend,' she whispered. It was not the whole answer. She did not know the whole answer herself.

She risked a glance away from the beast and looked up at her falcon. He had been watching all this time, eyes fixed on her, wings flickering in a frenzy. *You know who I am*, she thought. But it wasn't yet time to ask.

Leave me now, she told her Peregrine, and it took more courage to let him go than she had ever had to summon before. **Take Gar home – he needs to keep Ma safe.**

In reply, her falcon spiralled swift from the sky. He hovered over Gar's head, the beat of his wings lifting the boy's black hair in greeting, and then he skimmed away over the marsh. Showing Gar the way.

'*Airk! Airk!*'

'Follow him, Gar. Run! I can't hold back this creature for long.'

And without a backwards glance – no matter how much it hurt him to obey – Gar left Rhodd and ran.

CHAPTER 35

The beast brooded over the desolation it had created about itself. To Rhodd's relief, it had watched Gar go and not stirred. But, of course, it had her in its power instead. And that was what it had wanted for so long.

It seemed a strange thing, to have to make small talk with an animal as ancient as the earth. But it was only Rhodd's gift for speaking to creatures that could make her plan work and save the wild world now.

Can I keep it talking until Gar gets them away from the village? Rhodd was asking herself. How long would it take for him to get back there, and persuade them all of the danger? She knew Ma and Bethan would listen at least. And part of her didn't care about the rest of them.

'It's their own lookout,' she whispered to herself but

she knew that was wrong.

Anyway, there was an even bigger problem facing her. How to persuade this thing to do her bidding and wash away the marsh? It was not clever enough to argue with, it did not have the words . . . all it had was anger.

Rhodd looked out over the desolate waste, the dead reeds, the decaying grass. The water was stagnant but it seethed with the offspring of the creature. Even if this bitter creature died, there would be more to take its place. It would not be enough to kill it – even if she wanted to. This was a possessed and poisoned land, where once the river had flowed wide and free to the sea.

She tried to imagine what it had once looked like, the blue of reflected sky, the crimson and gold of the setting sun, a silver path of moonlight . . . the cries of a thousand sea birds wheeling overhead . . .

It was beautiful. The answer was coming from the beast. It was listening to her mind-shapes and was full of longing. **I loved the river. Men took it from me.**

Rhodd stared into its grim face. The pupils were still narrow slits, the mouth clamped closed in ominous threat. At any moment it could decide to finish what it had tried to do all those years before. And she would end up as another little pile of bones on the mud.

It was just one man. A bad man, she told the beast. **Greedy. And stupid.** The beast felt at the shapes of those ideas in its mind but she knew that 'bad' was the only bit it understood.

She tried again. **You were angry.** And then she regretted that, because the answer was a great rumble of fury that threatened to spill out of control. **You are still angry.** She bowed her head. **I understand.** She told it again, **I am angry too.**

It was mine! The river was mine. The beast spat venom, narrowly missed Rhodd. **Man stole it.**

The coils of the creature's body tightened and the whole marsh shuddered. What strength this beast had . . . if only she could use it . . .

So what did you do? Anything to keep it talking.

I seized it back. Wrapped myself around it.

The mouth gaped open and the black-forked tongue spilled out and flickered over the space between them. She felt hot breath singeing the hairs on her skin, the heat of the fires stoking up inside it. She looked desperately to the sky for her falcon. Would he come back to tell her when Ma was safe? He had never been hers to command, but . . .

For the moment, all she could do was keep the beast calm. It was too soon to unleash its fury.

You wanted to protect it. Because you loved it. Soothing it. Buying herself time. She felt the anger subsiding.

Rhodd changed the subject. **Why did you kill the children?**

The beast's mood changed again.

Hungry. It was sulky now. Defensive.

But children? Why children? Why not take men?

Rhodd had no love for the children who had bullied her and Gar. But she had grown up in that village and she knew that their cruelty had come from their parents. And their parents' cruelty had started with the death of the river and grown with the creep of the marsh.

To hurt. Children were blood payment. Revenge.

Why one a year? Rhodd was probing its dark mind for answers. **Why always in the spring?**

Spring is new life. My river was dead. Children are new life.

Then it said again simply, **Revenge.**

Rhodd did not bother to ask why two boys this year. Anger was all this creature had left – and the anger had grown out of its own control. It was trapped here, with no hope of escape to the sea – its coils and its spawn had spread so that there was no longer room for it to move, barely room for it to breathe. It would keep taking life. Unless she stopped it.

But there was one question Rhodd had to ask, though she wasn't sure she wanted to hear the answer. **Did you kill them all – all the children?**

A long pause. The great head swivelled and the forked black tongue slithered over the hoard of pathetic bones. It was as if it was counting them.

It turned back to stare at Rhodd. Defiant. **There was one. Different.**

Rhodd hardly dared ask. **How was he different?**

I did not call him. The *sea* called him. He was hungry. Hungry for life.

'Rhys,' Rhodd whispered to herself. But there was still one big question. **So what did you do?**

I let him walk on to the sea. He loved the river. Like me. Big sadness in him.

Rhodd breathed again. This creature had let Rhys pass. If only she could see Ma once more, if only she could tell her that her son had not died that night – that he might still be alive.

But she needed to keep it talking.

You too are sad. Perhaps if she could remind it of what it had lost?

The beast stared at her balefully. It did not respond.

You wrapped your coils around the river and turned the earth to mud and marsh . . . Rhodd was searching for the right mind-shapes. **You bound it to you . . . to keep it safe . . . but now it binds you. You are trapped here. This place has become your prison.**

She had gone too far. She had touched on the truth, the truth of the beast's loneliness and despair. The marsh lurched beneath her feet and the silt swirled around her.

Why did you come back? I had you once before! You should have stayed away!

The huge head reared up, towering into the sky its muscular body unravelled from the marsh. It shook a torrent of mud from its scales. She could see it now; this creature had once been a glorious sea-serpent, swimming proud and free through the oceans. Until its anger trapped it in this place.

Why should I listen any longer?

The words came as a roar from its dark mind and Rhodd gasped as a huge hood spread wide behind its head and blocked out the light.

The blackness it brought with it was like night falling on the day. All Rhodd could see was the great mouth opening and the forked tongue hissing down at her. Poison dripped and burned on her limbs.

Too soon, too soon! thought Rhodd desperately, brushing the filthy stuff from her skin. She peered past the darkness for her falcon. But the sky was empty.

You grovelled like a worm on your belly . . . I had you in my jaws . . . but you escaped . . .

For the first time the memory of that fight flooded back to Rhodd. Struggling, hitting out with her little fists, kicking at a terrible creature whilst it stung her and tore at her legs with its fangs. But she had been so small and it had been so strong . . . How had she escaped?

Rhodd closed her eyes because she could almost feel those jaws closing around her again.

My falcon saved me.

She was saying the words as much to herself as to the beast. She was seeing again the moment when her Peregrine had flown at the beast and torn at its eyes with its talons. Now, Rhodd opened her own eyes and looked up.

And there her Peregrine was, hovering above her, like a twist of smoke before the wind. This was not memory.

They are safe, he told her. **It is time for you to fight.**

CHAPTER 36

Falcon eyes showed Rhodd what she had been desperate to see.

A long line of villagers was trudging up the road, away from their homes. Somehow Gar must have persuaded them to listen to him and leave, even before they were evicted by Lord Stanley.

And there – on the top of the cliff above the village – she saw Ma and Bethan and Gar. Together. Safe. Cerys was propped up with pillows and Bethan was swathing her in blankets. Red was resting his heavy head on her knees.

Ma was gazing out over the marsh. Not for the first time, Rhodd wondered what those wise eyes were looking at. *Can she see me?* For a brief moment, Rhodd longed for the safety of those beloved arms, folded about her like the wings of a swan.

But Rhodd could not let herself look for long. She had to face her last battle with this creature that had grown so strong – yet so warped – in its anger. She did not hope for survival. If she harnessed this power, it would likely destroy her and the beast both.

She stood tall and looked up.

I do not fear you now. I am no longer some small child for you to torture and terrify.

The sea-serpent fell back for a moment. And then it reared higher into the sky, showering Rhodd with years of stinking mud.

Rhodd's belly turned to water but she did not stop. **You are killing the wild-ness,** she told it.

She felt an answering surge of fury in its mind. A flash of longing for all that lost beauty.

The man killed the river! The beast lifted its head and roared fire out over the place that it had made its own. Flames belched from its smouldering belly, lighting the overcast skies with an eerie glow.

Rhodd could not look at it. Fire was the element she had always feared above all things, and now she remembered why. Robbed of its prey, this creature had turned his flames on her as she fled from the wild-ness all those years before.

Her scars were the scorches and stings it inflicted on her as she ran.

How could she ever hope to control *fire*?

Rhodd began to back away whilst she thought. But she needed to see what was behind her or she would end up being sucked into a gully.

Help me! I can't see!

Her falcon spiralled down from the sky and she saw again the whole marsh laid out around her. The flat expanse was writhing as the sea-serpent stirred up its spawn and the mud glowed blood-red from the reflected flames.

'Control the beast, control the beast!' Rhodd muttered to herself, under her breath. After struggling to keep the beast calm, now she must whip up its rage and use it to carry out her will. The fire wasn't enough. She needed it to loosen its coils and release its grip on the marsh. So that the sea could flow in once more.

She had to make it even angrier.

Look around you. You have killed the wild world in your anger, she taunted it. **You killed all those innocent creatures.**

Rhodd started to run backwards towards the village, trying to keep her face turned towards the serpent. Above her head, flames belched from its mouth and it bent its snaking head this way and that, following her every move, relentless. Poised to strike.

With the eyes of her falcon, Rhodd danced around the shifting banks of the gullies, light-footed. It was starting to work – the beast was having to unwrap more and more of its coils from the mud in order to follow her. But it was taking all her concentration to stop it from tripping her, trapping her.

And then, from nowhere, the serpent shook its great tail free from the slime. It whipped up and seized her.

Got you!

Rhodd felt the squeeze of the muscular tail as it writhed and wrapped itself around her ribs. She screamed in agony. She was being stabbed to death from the inside by her own broken bones. All the breath was being crushed from her body.

The grip grew tighter, tighter and the fearsome sting lashed at her legs, opening up old wounds. She felt herself being lifted from the mud towards the hissing mouth.

Rhodd braced herself for the attack, the tearing of its fangs into her flesh. The blast of flames. This time she would not survive.

I have failed. I'm sorry, she called out in despair to whatever was listening. **I wasn't strong enough to fight it.**

Now the river would never return, and the marsh would never be washed away.

Fangs were bared in her face. Rhodd smelled the stench of the beast's rotting breath.

This time you die.

Her last thought was that Ma would die never knowing that Rhys was still alive.

She shut her eyes and braced herself to face the fire.

CHAPTER 37

Keep fighting, child.

This was not the voice of her Peregrine. This was the voice that had kept her going on that cliff. The voice that had spoken to her on the night of her spirit-flight.

Hafren. The name formed its shape in Rhodd's mind and sent shivers of recognition through her. This was no myth. The goddess of the river was with her.

Yes, child. I am with you. Hafren's voice was pure joy to Rhodd – even now, just seconds from the beast's jaws.

Help me! Rhodd could smell the scorch of her own hair in the beast's breath.

Take my courage. You must complete your task.

And Rhodd opened her eyes and dared to taunt the beast once more.

You are as bad as that man, she told it.

Fire roared in the beast's belly. But at that moment an arrow of vengeance flew from the clouds and plunged, hind talons first, into its right eye.

The creature pulled back its huge head as it recoiled in agony, and the flames roared impotent into the air. It snapped at the air, trying to find its attacker.

But the Peregrine was already soaring away. *'Airk-Airk-Airk!'*

The tail lost its hold on Rhodd. She tumbled to the soft mud below and wriggled away, wrenching her ribs. But the sea-serpent swivelled its head. She was still its prey.

Rhodd hauled herself on to her feet and set her hands on her hips, elbows jutting in defiance. She had to make it so angry that it stopped thinking about her and unleashed all its mighty power.

You have betrayed your river, Rhodd told it.

The beast roared. And the roar shook the marsh and the dead, imprisoned river and echoed up into the blue distant hills.

And then Rhodd conjured the power of that name.

You have betrayed Hafren – the goddess of your river.

With another great roar, the beast's chest inflated to an immense size and great wings unfurled from its back.

They were wings grown withered from long disuse, but they were strong enough to beat the stale air into a gale.

Rhodd was struggling to stand, but she hurled her mind-shapes at the beast.

Use your anger, she commanded it. **Now! Use it to free the river. And free yourself!**

Rhodd darted out of the way as the beast harnessed wind and flame into a great ball of fire that torched the dry reeds and yellow grasses and tore across the dead marsh towards the village.

She held her breath as the fire leaped like a tiger over the quayside and the houses and licked hungrily at the red cliffs. But the flames could not reach the villagers above. Ma and Bethan and Gar and Red were safe.

The Peregrine soared up, away from the heat of the inferno and still Rhodd urged the beast on.

Rise up now! Release this foul marsh.

In its fury, the creature forgot Rhodd as its wings stirred up the mud and its vast coils burst the binding roots of the grasses. It was destroying the place it had created, the marsh that stood between land and sea.

Freed from the sea-serpent's coils, the silt flowed like water. The mud was dissolving beneath Rhodd's feet. She had been looking inland but now she turned towards the sea. And gasped.

A great tidal wave was gathering there, as if all the waters of the oceans had been waiting for this moment. Too late, Rhodd realised her own danger. But she was curiously free from fear.

For on the white crest of that huge wave rode the most beautiful woman she had ever seen. It was her chariot and the waves surging before it were her horses. Her hair streamed down like a shaft of sunlight, her face shone clear as the rising moon, and her robes flowed in the crashing surf.

Hafren! Rhodd cried. This was the princess who had been taken by the river and transformed into a goddess. This was what men had called myth – now made real. The goddess was returning to reclaim her lost home. The river that Rhodd had saved.

Hafren cried back to Rhodd, **My daughter! My beloved child . . . You have done well!**

With those words, Rhodd knew at last who she was. She was the daughter of Hafren.

Mother!

Quickly, follow me, child! The river is returning!

Hafren's chariot swept on and the wall of water crashed down towards Rhodd.

She looked up and her Peregrine was carving through the air towards her.

Fly! he told her. **It is time.**

And Rhodd left behind her scarred and broken body and rose up into the blood and bones and feathers of her falcon. It was – at last – what she had always longed for; the rush of the wind beneath her wings and the freedom of the sky.

And together they followed the path of Hafren's chariot.

Rhodd soared with her Peregrine over the great wave as it crashed towards the land. The surge burst the man-made banks of the canal and the salt waters flowed in and washed away the last of the marsh mud.

Below them, the sea-serpent was engulfed. For a moment it struggled to lift its head and free itself from the chaos of its own making. But then finally, it rose out of the swirling waters and roared its triumph to the skies before sinking back into the sea. Its spawn scattered to seek their own freedom in the ocean.

And Rhodd and her Peregrine flew on, over the wild world.

The sun had broken through the heavy clouds. It was the loveliest of days.

How can I bear to leave all this behind? Rhodd was

thinking of that other mother, the Ma who had wrapped her arms about her like a swan and kept her safe. And Gar, the friend who had been by her side every step of the way until he could follow her no further.

You will not leave it, came the answer. **We will always fly together and be part of it, part of the earth and the sea and the skies . . . and the spirits of all creatures . . .**

And Rhodd dared at last to ask her falcon the question she had never asked.

Who are you?

I am Hafren's spirit and I have watched over you always. You had a task to do and you have done it.

And now? Rhodd asked.

And now I am sent to bring you home to your mother. And to the river.

EPILOGUE

A Peregrine soared . . .

. . . over a river, winding wild through ancient grassy banks studded with golden dandelions and buttoned with daisies . . .

. . . over tumbling, teeming skies full of whirring wings and feathers, alive with calls and cries and chattering and song . . .

. . . over green hills and fields where rabbits grazed and skylarks rose singing from the earth, bringing with their music the smell of sunshine and new grass and sweet primroses in the spring . . .

. . . over a black-haired boy walking away from a village and never looking back, swinging a bag of books and whistling with the promise of a new life at the end of his journey . . .

. . . over a mother with a letter in her hand, running like a girl, lightsome and unheartbroken – and waiting on tiptoe at a bustling quayside . . .

. . . out over the sea where white sails, unfurled to the wind, told of a ship carrying home a long-lost son . . .

And the Peregrine flew on, shrieking a wild skirling cry that was part deep joy and part terrible sadness . . .

'*Airk! Airk!*'

Rhodd was falcon, she was Peregrine, she was the daughter of Hafren who had been sent to save the wild . . . and she rose up and was lost in a rent in the sky.

AUTHOR'S NOTE

I grew up on the edge of a wild marsh, watching the sun set in the west each night over its brooding presence; beyond the marsh there was the glint of a shining river and the distant promise of the sea.

The marsh was a place of mystery and menace. There was talk that those in the know could find the old paths between its treacherous channels and all the way to Wales – another country, its distant hills the beautiful blue of possibility and a life beyond. My brother was one of those in the know, of course – he was a distant four years older; I never dared to follow him.

Between our house and the marsh, in those times, lay fields and ponds and hedgerows where we children roamed free. Wild flowers buzzed with insects; skylarks soared skywards, startled, from their hidden nests on the earth. During those everlasting summers we made dens in the long grass and fished for newts and sticklebacks in jam-jars tied at the neck with string, and looked on with silent envy at anyone lucky enough to capture such a prized beast.

And then came the bulldozers and the bricklayers; a brief interlude brought a new playground of deep clay-filled trenches where a wellington boot could be sucked down in seconds, never to be seen again. In one short winter, the fields and the ponds and the hedgerows and all the creatures and birds and insects were gone, replaced by tarmacked roads and neat little houses and neat little cars that brought new dangers and curtailed our former freedom.

It became the stuff of myth, for me, that marsh. I grew up knowing only that once a great river had flowed here, fast and free, bringing ships from all over the world; but then the marsh came and took the river away. I always thought I could be the one to bring it back. Maybe, in *Wilder*, that is what I have tried to do.

Perhaps, for me, *Wilder* is a lament for a lost way of life. But I hope it is also a rallying call for us all to fight for the wild places and the wild creatures, before they are all lost to us for ever.

ACKNOWLEDGEMENTS

This book would not be a book if it wasn't for all those who have loved and fought for our wild world and kept the special spaces safe for us all to go to find our souls.

I spent a lot of time at Elmley Nature Reserve on the Isle of Sheppey, where Gareth and Georgina have continued her parents' pioneering work on habitat and biodiversity. Nothing quite so wonderful as falling asleep listening to the call of owls across the water.

And also at the RSPB reserves at Burton Mere and Parkgate on the Dee estuary on the Wirral, where inspired conservation has restored the marshes beyond which the sun sinks so gloriously into the sea.

So many thanks are due to my editor, Lena McCauley, for all her passionate support; to Ruth Girmatsion, copy-editor Jenny Glencross, proof-reader Cat Phipps. And of course, to illustrator Manuel Šumberac and the wonderful design team including Jennifer Alliston at Hachette Children's Group who have made *Wilder* into such a beautiful book. Also to Namishka Doshi and Katie Maxwell from PR and Marketing for all their hard work.

And last – but never least – to my agent, Lisa Babalis at Curtis Brown, who helped me with unfailing support and friendship through a difficult year.

Fly never meant to end up in a cage with a tiger.
And though she's sure she's no princess, when the
tiger addresses her as 'your majesty', she can't help
but vow to free him and return him home.

A magical tale of a bold young chimney sweep,
a remarkable tiger and a mystical land found across
an ocean and through a storm.

ONE MAGICAL
FRIENDSHIP

ONE ROARING
ADVENTURE

Tiger
Heart

PENNY CHRIMES

When Stick discovers an ancient dragon trapped in a
tunnel underneath London, he's more than a bit
scared. Nonetheless he decides to help her, if he can.

A fiery adventure about a dragon (who loves
crumpets), a boy (with a secret in his past),
and the friendship that saves them both.

The
Dragon
and
Her **Boy**

PENNY CHRIMES

After working in Fleet Street,
Penny Chrimes was a television news
journalist for most of her career.
She now lives in Kent and writes full time.
She is the author of two books about the
gutterling children of London, *Tiger Heart*
and *The Dragon and her Boy*.

Find her on Twitter
@pennychrimes